ROCKE1

In memory of my father,
Bud Ashby
—R. A.

Ω
Published by
PEACHTREE PUBLISHERS
1700 Chattahoochee Avenue
Atlanta, Georgia 30318-2112
www.peachtree-online.com

Book design by Adela Pons
Composition by Adela Pons

Photographs and official NASA patches and emblems courtesy of National Aeronautics and Space Administration (NASA) and Johnson Space Center

Printed in February 2019 in the United States of America by LSC Communications in Harrisonburg, Virginia
10 9 8 7 6 5 4 3 2 (hardcover)
10 9 8 7 6 5 4 3 2 1 (trade paperback)

HC ISBN: 978-1-56145-323-8
PB ISBN: 978-1-68263-104-1

Library of Congress Cataloging-in-Publication Data

Ashby, Ruth.
Rocket man : the Mercury adventure of John Glenn / written by Ruth Ashby ; illustrated by Robert Hunt.— 1st ed.
p. cm.
ISBN 978-1-56145-323-4
1. Project Mercury (U.S.)—History—Juvenile literature. 2. Glenn, John, 1921—Juvenile literature.
I. Hunt, Robert, 1952– ill. II. Title.
TL789.8.U6M4137 2004
629.45'0092—dc22

2004005549

ROCKET MAN

The Mercury Adventure of John Glenn

RUTH ASHBY

PEACHTREE
ATLANTA

Table of Contents

Author's Note

John Glenn was my childhood hero. I still remember sitting in my elementary school cafeteria to watch his Mercury flight on the school's one black-and-white TV. Glenn's reentry into the atmosphere was edge-of-the-seat suspenseful, since the TV audience knew before he did that the heat shield might be down. I loved Glenn because of his courage and daring but also because he reminded me of my father—another bald, handsome ex-Marine who had fought in the South Pacific and was nicknamed "Bud." To this day I cannot see Glenn's picture without thinking of my dad.

To write this book, I relied primarily on John Glenn's own memoir, the astronauts' collective account, *We Seven*, and a transcript of the actual *Friendship 7* flight. I took dialogue verbatim from the transcript and, in a few instances, from Glenn's book as well. One of the best accounts of the Mercury Project is Tom Wolfe's brilliant book, *The Right Stuff*. It was made into an excellent movie that older children as well as adults can enjoy.

—R. A.

Rocket Man

It was one-thirty in the morning, February 20, 1962. John Glenn was wide-awake in his bunk in the crew quarters at Cape Canaveral, Florida. Today was the day. He was finally going into space, after three years of training—and waiting.

It would all come down to the next few hours.

Ever since Glenn had been chosen as a Mercury astronaut in America's brand-new space program, his life had been on fast forward. He'd loved every minute of training, from the sessions in the flight simulator to the meetings with President John Kennedy.

The only thing he didn't like were the endless delays. Glenn's flight had already been canceled ten times, mostly on account of bad weather. Once he had even waited in the tiny space capsule for five hours, before

Mission Control told him to get out and go home. But he refused to think about another delay now.

He began to go over flight procedures in his head, one more time.

Half an hour later the crew doctor, Dr. William Douglas, came in to see Glenn. The weather was iffy, Douglas reported. Maybe it would clear up. Maybe it wouldn't.

Glenn could only hope for the best. He got up and shaved and showered. Breakfast was a super-energy astronaut special: steak and eggs, toast with jelly, orange juice, and high grain cereal. Then the doctor gave him a quick exam.

"You're fit to go," Douglas said. He began sticking little metal biosensors onto Glenn's body. They would keep track of his heart rate, blood pressure, and temperature while he was in orbit.

Next came the pressure suit. Glenn put on the undergarment first, two layers of heavy mesh with metal coils sandwiched between them. Air flowing through the coils would control his temperature during the flight. Then he climbed into the silver suit and zipped up its thirteen zippers. He felt in a pocket for the five little American flags and the special pins he had designed picturing a space capsule circling the Earth.

They would make good souvenirs of his flight, Glenn thought. He could give them to his two young children, and to the president.

As Glenn put on his silver boots, Douglas stuck the hose from the air supply tube into a fish tank. He figured that if the air was bad, the fish would sense it and react. Glenn, who always liked a good joke, decided to give the doctor a scare. He went over and peered into the tank.

"Hey, Bill," he called out. "Did you know a couple of those fish are floating belly-up?"

"What?" Douglas exclaimed. He rushed over, expecting to find some dead fish. He grinned when he saw the fish swimming around happily. The doctor was glad to see that Glenn was in such good spirits. He shook the astronaut's hand and wished him a good voyage.

Glenn stuck his white helmet on his head and took the transport van over to the launch pad. He stepped out onto a dramatic scene. It looked like a movie set, with floodlights playing on the towering Atlas missile. Glenn himself, in his shining silver suit, could have been a visitor from another planet. Today he would become a true astronaut, a sailor among the stars.

Glenn walked into the elevator and rode the six stories up to the capsule. Fellow astronaut Scott Carpenter, his backup for this mission, was waiting in the "white room" at the top. The room was sterile and dust free. Carpenter and the rest of the crew wore white jump suits and white paper caps on their heads. Glenn joked that it made them look like old-fashioned drugstore soda boys.

The crew would stuff him, feet first, into the capsule. The name *Friendship 7* had been painted in red and white on its side: friendship for world peace, seven for the seven Mercury astronauts. Glenn's own children, Dave and Lyn, had picked out the name. He thought it was perfect.

By 6:06 A.M., Glenn was in the capsule. *Friendship 7* was tiny, just ten feet high and six feet wide at its base. Being inside felt like being crammed into a telephone booth, except that Glenn couldn't turn around. The seat had been molded to his back and fit him like a great body glove. He was packed in so tightly he could barely move his fingers, let alone anything else.

The capsule was bolted shut. The countdown started. T minus 60 minutes.

Through his helmet headset, Glenn could hear the chatter at Mission Control. They were talking about the thickening clouds. The countdown clock stopped. Not again, he thought, thinking of all the other delays.

A while later, the clouds thinned out. The countdown resumed.

Glenn looked out the periscope that gave him a view of the outside world. Far below him the waves broke on the Florida shore. Down the beach, way off in the distance, he could see the thousands of people who had come to watch his liftoff. Some had been there for a month, waiting out the delays. The whole country— the whole world—was eager for the moment John Glenn would be blasted into space.

But no one was more eager than Glenn!

T minus 35 minutes. Crew members filled up the rocket booster tanks with liquid oxygen, or *lox*. There were eighty tons of lox in the Atlas, kept at a temperature of 293 degrees below zero. The extreme cold made the metallic shell of the missile bend and shiver. Perched on top of the immense machine, Glenn could feel it shake and thump beneath him.

T minus 22 minutes. A rocket valve stuck. The countdown stopped, then began again.

T minus 6 minutes. Another holdup, and another fresh start.

Sixty seconds and counting. Across America, people edged closer to their black-and-white television sets and fixed their eyes on the screen.

Glenn held his breath.

It was really going to happen. In a few moments, the great Atlas rocket would lift into the air, and *Friendship 7* would be shot into space. For the first time, the United States would have a man in orbit around the Earth. And John Glenn, small-town hero from New Concord, Ohio, would be that man.

CHAPTER ONE

All-American Boy

Y ou want to go up, Bud?" Herschel Glenn asked his eight-year-old son. He pointed to a small plane parked out on a grassy field. Its pilot leaned casually against a wing, waiting for passengers.

Young John—his father called him Bud—couldn't believe his luck. He was going to get a chance to fly! In 1929, an airplane was still a strange and marvelous sight. Just two years earlier, fellow Ohio native Charles Lindbergh had thrilled the world by making the first solo flight across the Atlantic Ocean. He came back to brass bands and ticker tape parades, an instant hero. Soon afterwards John had spotted a silver plane far overhead, winging its way through the soft summer sky, and imagined it was Lindbergh. That plane was the most beautiful thing John had ever seen.

The one he was about to ride in now was a biplane.

It had two wings, one stacked on top of the other, and two cockpits. The pilot helped John and his father into the rear seat. Then he climbed into the front and started the engine. The plane started off, bumping over the ground. It picked up speed—and rose into the air.

So this was flying! John peered over the edge of the plane and saw the Ohio countryside spread out beneath him. White farmhouses, red barns, and tiny black-and-white cows dotted the patchwork fields. The wind whistling past his head filled him with energy and excitement. He wanted to stay up in the sky forever! But after just a few more loops, the ride was over.

For John, that first flight was the beginning of a life-long dream. He knew then that he would do *anything* to become a pilot. He would just have to wait for the right opportunity to come along.

John Herschel Glenn Jr. was born on July 18, 1921. His hometown of New Concord, Ohio, was a small place with only a thousand people and no traffic lights. Its busy downtown boasted a firehouse, a bank, two Presbyterian churches, six grocery stores, two ice cream parlors, two hardware stores, and a number of other businesses. John's father Herschel owned a plumbing business on Main Street, where his mother

All-American Boy

Clara helped out. When little Bud was a toddler, he would sit on the floor of the store and play by the hour with the copper plumbing pipes. To take a nap, he curled up in a porcelain tub.

Once a month Bud's parents got together with four other couples for a potluck supper. When he was two or three, they put him into a playpen with a dark-haired little girl just a year older. Her name was Annie Castor, and the two children became good friends. At age five, Bud welcomed a little girl into his own family, an adopted daughter the Glenns named Jean.

Later Glenn would remember his childhood as just about perfect. New Concord was heaven for a small boy, with woods to explore and creeks to fish in. With the rest of his friends, red-haired, freckle-faced Bud went ice-skating in the winter and on Sunday school picnics and hayrides in the summer.

Every patriotic holiday, the town would get together to celebrate America. On the Fourth of July, there would be ice cream and lemonade, firecrackers and Roman candles lighting up the evening sky. On Armistice Day, veterans of the First World War and the Spanish American War and even a few old soldiers from the Civil War paraded down Main Street, cheered on by spectators waving American flags.

One Memorial Day, families visited the cemetery

as usual to honor servicemen who had died for their country. Raising his trumpet to his lips, Herschel Glenn began to play "Taps," the traditional military call that signals the end of the day and the end of life. John stood with his own trumpet in the nearby woods, hidden among the trees. As each musical phrase rang into the still air, he echoed it. Back and forth the trumpets sounded, until the last note died away. The ceremony was so moving that John felt chills down his spine.

In 1929 a shadow fell across America, stretching from New York to California and over the little town of New Concord. The shadow was called the Great Depression. That fall, the stock market plummeted, and the country was swept by financial panic. Banks went broke. People lost their jobs and their savings. Many didn't have the money to buy food, clothes, or cars—or to get their plumbing repaired. Most of Herschel Glenn's customers couldn't pay him in cash. Sometimes they sent him a cut of beef or a few hams instead.

One night Bud overheard his mother and father talking in whispers. They might lose the house, his father said. If the Glenns couldn't make their monthly loan payments, the bank would take the house back.

Lose their house? Bud felt a jolt of fear. He knew that lots of folks were becoming homeless during the Depression. He decided he would do anything he could to make sure his family kept a roof over their heads.

That meant he had to do a job he hated—gardening. The Glenns had three garden plots, and John cleared, hoed, and planted them all. In summer and fall, he picked peas, beans, tomatoes, and corn. Clara Glenn would put the fruits and vegetables up in glass jars for the winter. One year they had a bumper crop of rhubarb. Bud washed and tied it up, put it on his wagon, and hawked it around town. One bundle sold for just a few pennies. Soon, Glenn remembered, "you could smell rhubarb pie baking all over town."

Sometimes Bud went rabbit hunting with his father and uncle. Like most boys living in rural areas, he had learned to use a shotgun early. Fresh rabbit stew was delicious.

Gardening and selling vegetables was a good way to earn money, but Bud looked for better and faster ways. Washing cars seemed like another surefire moneymaking scheme. Bud took out an ad in a local newspaper. It read: "Kars Cleaned Kwickly, Kompletely—50 cents." He saved all the money he earned for a bicycle. When he finally had sixteen dollars, he bought a secondhand bike with a wire basket on the handlebars. Soon young John Glenn was New Concord's number one paperboy.

The Glenn family finances began to improve when the new president, Franklin Delano Roosevelt, helped get the unemployed back to work. The Federal Works Progress Administration set up a program to install a new water system in New Concord. Because he was a plumber, Herschel Glenn was made a foreman on the project. Roosevelt's program to electrify rural America also helped Glenn's business. Once farmers had electricity, they could pump water into their houses and barns.

Yes, the Great Depression was hard. But it also brought out the can-do spirit in everyone, even the kids. Since there was no Boy Scout troop in town, Bud and his friends decided to form their own club, which they named the Ohio Rangers. They found an old Boy Scout handbook and practiced their camping skills. Their first campsite was a circle of pup tents with a flagpole in the center. Bud and his friends slept there nearly every night the summer he was twelve, roasting hot dogs on sticks and eating baked beans in cans. Then one night, the campsite was drowned out in a raging thunderstorm.

So the Rangers built a log cabin instead. On their

own, the boys chopped down small trees, cut them into logs, and notched them at the edges. Then they fitted the logs one on top of each other and packed the cracks with mud. A roof of pine branches kept out the rain and snow. The cabin was so small that only two boys could sleep in it at once—but it was a real log cabin nonetheless. It was quite an achievement for a bunch of twelve-year-olds.

When Glenn became a teenager, his love of camping gave way to a love of cars. By now his father had a second job as a Chevrolet dealer. John would spend hours working on a used car engine, taking it apart and putting it back together. His "tinkering became an education," he remembered.

When John was fifteen, he got his first driver's license. The next year, his father gave him his very own car, an old Chevrolet roadster with no top. John painted it bright red. He couldn't wait to show it to Annie, the childhood playmate who had become his girlfriend. They nicknamed it the "Cruiser." John wasn't always content to use his shiny red car just for transportation. Once after a rainstorm, he drove the Cruiser onto the high school football field and spun "doughnuts" on the squishy ground, the mud flying up over the wheels. He managed to damage the old car badly and had to spend the next few weeks fixing it up again.

Another one of John's favorite daredevil tricks was to "shoot" the old B&O railroad bridge. Even though it was a one-lane bridge, John would rev the engine and fly across it. Once he almost smashed into a car coming from the other direction—and never tried the stunt again.

John flew through high school, too. Always curious and super-competitive, he was an A student, president of the junior class, an actor in the school play, and a letterman in football, basketball, and tennis. "Whatever he did," a classmate remembered, "he put his whole self into it." John even got an A in his Boys' Home-Making course by baking a delicious chocolate fudge cake.

As junior class president, John got to pick the theme for the annual school banquet. He knew just what theme he wanted: aviation. By 1938, the airplane industry was booming and airplanes were appearing everywhere. A Ford Trimotor plane decorated the cover of the banquet booklet. Glenn and the senior class president proudly called themselves the class "pilots."

The title was purely wishful thinking, of course. John's dream of flying was alive, but it still seemed out of reach. The summer after high school he and his father went to Cleveland for the National Air Races.

All day John watched daredevil pilots cruise the skies, his mouth open in wonder. There was aerobatic stunt flying, parachute jumping, and sailplane gliding. The high point was a speed race—thirty laps around a ten-mile course—won by the hottest hotshot pilot of them all, Roscoe Turner. When John spied Turner in his goggles and dashing leather flight suit, he was inspired all over again. But flying lessons were really expensive. He could not imagine ever being able to pay for them.

After high school, John enrolled at nearby Muskingum College. Annie Castor was already there, studying in the music department. Annie was a smart, outgoing girl with dark brown eyes and a brilliant smile. She also had a very bad stutter. But John had known Annie so long he barely noticed the way she talked. The stutter was just a part of her.

John and Annie already knew they wanted to get married some day. Sometimes they were so impatient that they dreamed of running away to Kentucky for a quick wedding ceremony. But they knew they had to get their college degrees first. It sure seemed a long time to wait.

The world had changed by the time John and Annie entered Muskingum. Far away in Europe, a war was raging. German chancellor Adolf Hitler and his Nazi party had stormed across the continent, intent on world domination. German soldiers marched into Czechoslovakia and Poland in 1939, then through Denmark, Norway, Holland, Belgium, and France. By fall 1940, only Britain was standing firm against the German peril. High in the skies over the British Channel, British pilots in their Spitfires were waging a heroic fight against German ME-109s.

The United States had not yet entered the war. But President Roosevelt was lending Britain whatever aid he could, short of actually sending ground troops. The US military, though, was already gearing up for possible combat.

John was paying close attention to events overseas, never thinking that they might have anything to do with him—yet. Then, in January 1941, he spotted a notice on the college physics department bulletin board. The Civilian Pilot Training Program was looking for qualified students. Those accepted would learn how to fly an airplane—for free!

This was the answer to John Glenn's prayers.

CHAPTER TWO

Up, Up, and Away

John excitedly scanned the notice on the bulletin board. The Civilian Pilot Training Program, he read, was sponsored by the US government. Not only would participants receive all their training free, but they would also get college credit for physics.

Wow, John thought. This was just what he'd dreamed of. He couldn't wait to tell his mom and dad the great news.

Clara and Herschel Glenn, however, were not happy when John informed them that he wanted to become a pilot. "I'm not in favor of it, Bud," his father said immediately. "It's too dangerous."

The Glenns knew that pilots were often injured or killed in plane crashes in those days. Flying was the last thing they wanted their beloved only son to be doing.

John figured he needed to bring in some outside support. He invited Dr. Paul Martin, the program's sponsor at Muskingum College, over to his house to talk to his parents. Doc Martin told the Glenns that aviation was an up-and-coming industry. As a trained pilot, John would have his pick of careers—in commercial airlines or in the military.

Reluctantly, Clara and Herschel agreed. John quickly applied to the program before they could change their minds. He was immediately accepted.

April 1941 found Glenn and three classmates at the pilot training center in New Philadelphia, Ohio. They had already done the preliminary academic work, studying up on subjects such as aerodynamics and airplane instruments. Now they were ready to start actual flight training.

Their first plane was a little Taylorcraft that could reach ninety miles per hour. The instructor sat beside Glenn in the enclosed cockpit. At first the instructor took the plane up. He allowed John to take the controls and practice wide, slow turns. After more experience, the instructor permitted him to guide the takeoff, increasing speed until the plane lifted off the ground and climbed into the sky.

Soon the small, light craft felt like an extension of

Glenn's own body. He learned to do wide, lazy S curves and tight figure eights, to make quick touchdowns and forced emergency landings. I think I'm going to be good at this, Glenn told himself.

In just three months he had his pilot's license. The first thing he wanted to do was show off his new skills to his father.

So one day he rented a small plane at a nearby airfield. As Herschel Glenn climbed into the cockpit next to his son, the plane sank down. John knew this was potential trouble. Herschel was a big man, 230 pounds, and the plane was near its weight limit. Would they be able to get off the ground?

Sure enough, the plane had difficulty picking up speed. The runway was fairly short, with a clump of trees at the end. John could see the trees loom larger as they sped down the runway.

The trees got closer, and closer...

Faster! John urged the plane. Go faster!

Beside him, Herschel sat tight-lipped, his hands gripping his seat.

At the last possible second, the plane lifted into the air—and skimmed the tops of the trees.

John let out his breath. His father turned to him with a grin. "Like those exciting takeoffs, do you?" he said.

In fall 1941, John was a college junior. Annie, a senior, had become an accomplished organist and was thinking about continuing her study of music in graduate school. The first Sunday in December, she was to give a solo organ recital at the Muskingum chapel. On his way to the recital, John was listening to the car radio when an emergency broadcast cut into the regularly scheduled show.

"The Japanese have bombed Pearl Harbor!" the newscaster announced.

Without warning, Japanese planes had attacked the US Naval fleet stationed at Pearl Harbor, Hawaii. In one day, Japanese bombers destroyed nineteen American ships and two hundred planes. The next day, President Roosevelt addressed Congress and asked them to declare war on Japan. December 7, 1941, he thundered, was a "date which will live in infamy!" Just three days later, Germany and Italy declared war on the United States. It looked as if Americans would be fighting on two fronts—in Europe and the Pacific Ocean—at the same time.

John knew where his duty lay. "I have to go," he told Annie when they were alone together. Somberly, she nodded. For patriotic John Glenn, there could be only one decision when his nation was in peril.

John dropped out of college. In April 1942, he was accepted to the US Navy preflight school. He had just one important thing to take care of before he left. He bought a sparkling little diamond ring and slipped it on Annie's finger. They were engaged.

Glenn was not ready to head overseas yet, though. It took a lot of training—at least a year's worth—to become a full-fledged military pilot. He needed athletic training to get in physical shape and academic training to be mentally prepared. He had to learn about engines, machine guns, aerodynamics, how to sight an enemy plane, and how to navigate by the stars.

Step by step Glenn learned to fly more powerful and sophisticated planes: Stearmans, open cockpit biplanes that could go 135 mph. Vultee Valiants, two-seaters that reached 180 mph. Big PBYs, or "flying boats," that cruised at 120 mph and could land on water.

Instructors tried all sorts of tricks to get cadet pilots ready for combat conditions. They would roll the plane upside down so that the engine would cut out and the plane would glide along without power. John got used to hanging upside down, fastened only by his seat belts. Or instructors would make cadets fly under hoods that blocked the view through the plane window, so that they had to navigate by instruments alone. This nerve-wracking exercise was called "flying blind."

Glenn met another young pilot, Tom Miller, who became his good friend. To Tom, John confided his greatest ambition—to be a fighter pilot. Fighters got to see all the real action.

Together the cadets vowed to do whatever it took to make the grade. The first step was to join the Marine Corps, a special branch of the Navy. Marines were known for their pride and loyalty and for never letting their buddies down. In the war in the Pacific, the Marines were taking back Japanese-held islands inch by inch. When ground troops landed on the islands, pilots helped protect them from the air. "Some of the Marines were coming back from the fighting there," Glenn remembered later, "telling stories of combat and bravery that made me want to join them."

What's more, the Marine Air Corps had the most powerful fighter jets around.

So after graduating from pre-flight school in the top ten percent of their class, John and Tom joined the Marines. In the short fifteen days before reporting for duty, John rushed back to New Concord for a special day. On April 6, 1943, John watched Annie come down the aisle on her father's arm, a radiant smile on her face. After twenty years of love and friendship, he and Annie were finally getting married.

When Glenn reported back to training camp, Annie came with him. It was at the air station in San Diego, California, that Glenn learned a hard lesson about life in the military. He and Tom wanted to join a fighter squadron that flew the newest, hottest planes: Corsairs. They begged the squadron's leader to let them in.

Okay, Major Haines said. But only if they got permission from their present commander, Major Zoney.

But Glenn was in a rush. He ignored Haines's advice and went straight to Zoney's superior, the lieutenant colonel in charge of the whole group. By going over Zoney's head, he had ignored the military chain of command. And, as he soon found out, he had made a major mistake.

Major Zoney was furious. "In this man's Marine Corps, you need to learn where orders come from," he barked at Glenn. "They come from your immediate superior. That's *me.*"

Glenn felt awful. He was sure he had ruined his chances to become a fighter pilot. He practically got down on his knees to apologize to Zoney. Finally, he got his transfer.

On February 5, 1944, Glenn and his squadron, the VMO-1555, were sent overseas. Saying good-bye to Annie was tough.

John tried to make light of the separation. "I'm just going down to the corner store to get a pack of gum," he said.

"Don't be long," Annie replied, trying not to cry.

During the long ocean voyage to Hawaii, Glenn discovered that he was prone to seasickness. He spent much of the trip hanging over the rail, feeling nauseated. He was grateful when they finally reached Honolulu. Immediately he found a hula outfit to send back home to Annie.

The first mission of the VMO-1555 was to protect the submarine base on Midway Island from Japanese bombers. At dawn and dusk every day, Glenn was in the "ready room," prepared for takeoff. When the alert siren blared, pilots raced out to the planes and jumped in the cockpits. Glenn's group called itself the "Ready Teddys." On the side of his Corsair was painted a running teddy bear in a flight suit.

Off duty, Glenn relaxed by playing volleyball and singing harmony with the guys. He also got a kick out of watching the local bird: the albatross, or gooney, as it was affectionately known. The gooney is one of nature's most graceful and athletic flyers.

On land, though, the gooney looks awkward and silly. Glenn would sit and chuckle as he watched one of the majestic birds come in for a dignified landing— only to "tumble beak over webbed feet in a cloud of dust."

Soon Glenn's squadron was tapped for bombing raids over the Marshall Islands. The Americans were moving steadily across the Pacific, capturing one island at a time from the Japanese. But too many American lives were being lost in ground attacks. The US opted for a bombing campaign instead.

In June 1944, the men and planes of VMO-1555 boarded an aircraft carrier, the USS *Makin Island*. A few days later, Glenn was in the cockpit of his Corsair on the deck of the carrier, a kind of floating runway. Glenn opened up the throttle, the catapult officer gave the signal, and the plane hurtled into the air. It was just like being shot out of a rubber band. Writing in his diary later, Glenn recorded that he was "out in space flying and not too sure how [he] got there."

A month later, Glenn, Tom Miller, and two other buddies were on a bombing mission over the Japanese island of Maloelap. Glenn and Miller were the leaders of the formation, with a pilot from Pennsylvania named Monte Goodman off Glenn's wing. Down they dived at 400 mph, trying to hit the target and get out before the Japanese could get them in their sights. But when the pilots regrouped at base after the run, Monte was missing. He had been shot down.

Shaken, Glenn went back over the ocean to look for his friend. But all he could find was an oil slick spreading over the dark water. Monte was the closest friend Glenn lost during the war. He never forgot that day.

The war in the Pacific was finally over in August 1945. By the end of the war, Glenn had flown fifty-nine missions and accumulated many honors: two Distinguished Flying Crosses and ten Air Medals. He went home to his proud family and thought about his next step. His father wanted him to take over his plumbing business. Annie's father, who was a dentist, suggested he try dentistry. But Glenn had seen the world and tasted danger. He didn't want to be land-bound—or New Concord–bound—again. He decided to stay in the Marines and keep on flying.

The vast blue skies were waiting.

CHAPTER THREE

Faster Than a Speeding Bullet

The next few years were busy ones for John and Annie Glenn. Now they had what they'd always wanted—two children of their own. John David (Dave) was born December 13, 1945, and Carolyn (Lyn) on March 15, 1947. Glenn wasn't able to spend as much time with his children as he would have liked, though. As a Marine captain, Glenn was often sent to the other side of the globe—to places like China, Okinawa, and Guam. Sometimes his growing family was able to accompany him—and sometimes they were not.

After the Korean War broke out, Glenn was assigned to combat duty again. In the frigid winter of 1953, he found himself in Korea piloting fighter-bombers, just as he had in World War II. His mission targets were railroads, bridges, supply depots, enemy troops—whatever command ordered.

That summer Glenn had a special goal—to become a fighter ace. Everybody knew that only the most daring pilots could engage the enemy in air-to-air combat. Glenn longed to prove he was one of them.

Soon enough, he made the grade. Flying the fastest plane of the war, the F86 Sabre, Glenn shot down three enemy MiGs in just nine days. "Today, finally got a MiG as cold as can be," he wrote home to his family after his first hit. "Of course, I'm not excited at this point. Not much!"

His dogfighting days did not last long, however. On July 27, 1953, a truce was declared. Glenn headed back to the States, and again he had to decide what to do. For an ambitious Marine pilot on his way up the military ladder, the most exciting choice was to become a test pilot.

Test pilots had the most dangerous aviation job of all. They had to try out new aircraft to make sure they were combat ready. Methodically, pilots would test each part of the plane: its electronics, its instruments, its weapons. Every day, they risked their lives. If a system did not work—well, it was a long way to the ground!

Glenn didn't know whether he would even qualify. After all, he had never even finished college, and most of the other test pilots were graduates of the Naval

Academy at Annapolis. Glenn realized he would have to work hard to make up for his lack of formal education. Night after night, he stayed up until the early morning hours studying algebra, trigonometry, and calculus. By sheer willpower, he passed the qualifying examinations.

It was not long before Glenn discovered how dangerous the job could be. One day he was flying out over the Atlantic Ocean, testing the firing capabilities of the FJ-3, the "Fury," when he heard a loud explosion.

The seal of the canopy had blown open! *Whoosh!* The air streamed out in a rush. Now Glenn was in a depressurized cabin eight miles above the ground.

Not only that, but he had no oxygen. He started gasping for breath.

Immediately he switched to his emergency oxygen backup. But then he found that the unthinkable had happened—the emergency system was broken, too!

Black patches began to float before Glenn's eyes. He knew he was about to lose consciousness.

Don't panic, he told himself. This was exactly the sort of desperate situation for which he'd been preparing ever since he had learned to fly.

He still had one hope left. All pilots kept a small extra bottle of oxygen in their parachute pack. Glenn put the plane into a steep dive and with one hand felt for the "little green apple"—a wooden ball connected by wire to the oxygen bottle—sticking out of the pack.

He had only seconds of consciousness left when his hand found the apple and pulled. Oxygen flooded into the hose leading to his helmet. He could breathe again!

Whew! It was a very close call.

One of the planes Glenn flew in those years was the F8U Crusader. The swiftest of the Navy fighter jets, it was able to reach supersonic speeds—faster than the speed of sound.

Glenn had a great idea. Ever competitive, he was always looking for a way to distinguish himself from other test pilots. He realized that the Crusader was the perfect plane to break the existing cross-country record of 3 hours and 45 minutes. The plane could actually go faster than a speeding .45 bullet, which shot out of a gun at "only" 586 mph. The Crusader, by contrast, had already set a speed record of 1,015 mph!

Project Bullet would be the perfect name for his cross-country race, Glenn decided.

Now all he had to do was convince the Navy brass that he was the man to break the record. It took a lot of persuading, but finally his permission came through.

The plan was to fly from the Los Alamitos Naval Air Station in California to Floyd Bennett Field in Brooklyn—2,445 miles across the continent. On July 16, 1957, Glenn strapped himself into the cockpit of the Crusader and set off.

Climbing swiftly up to 30,000—then 50,000—feet, Glenn reached a top speed of more than 1,000 mph. He could not maintain that astonishing pace, though, because the plane needed three refuelings along the way. At each pit stop, he had to reduce speed to 205 knots and drop down to 25,000 feet. The refueling was carried out in midair, with the Crusader hooked up to a large cargo plane.

As Glenn's supersonic plane streaked across the continent, a series of sonic booms exploded through the air. Sonic booms occur when an object exceeds the speed of sound. With each huge *boom!* windows far below shattered from the shock.

His flight path took him right above his hometown of New Concord. There the *boom-de-boom boom!* was so loud that one of Mrs. Glenn's neighbors called his mother. "Oh, Mrs. Glenn," the woman cried. "Johnny dropped a bomb! Johnny dropped a bomb!"

Glenn zoomed into Floyd Bennett Field with no fuel to spare. He had indeed set a cross-country record of

3 hours, 23 minutes and 8.4 seconds, at an average speed of 723 mph. Airplanes had certainly improved from the days when Glenn had chugged along in the old Taylorcraft—at 90 mph!

Annie, the Glenn children, and a crowd of reporters were waiting for him at the airport. The military sent him off on a publicity tour, which John thoroughly enjoyed. Besides appearing on TV and radio shows, he was a contestant on the game show *Name That Tune*. His partner was a ten-year-old boy named Eddie Hodges, who later starred in the musical *The Music Man* on Broadway. They made it through three rounds of the show—and won the prize!

Glenn did not expect to be in the public eye for long. A *New York Times* article made it clear that "At 36, Major Glenn is reaching the practical age limit for piloting complicated pieces of machinery through the air." Still, the celebrity was nice while it lasted.

Soon the nation's attention turned to more urgent matters. Just a few months after Glenn's flight, on October 4, 1957, the Soviet Union launched the first Earth satellite, a little steel spider named *Sputnik 1*. The American public was shocked—and a bit scared, too. The Russians had proved that their technology was superior. From space, Americans feared, the Communists could launch missiles at the United States. America had to catch up—and fast. Already, John Glenn's supersonic speed record seemed old-fashioned and unimportant. The new frontier would be not in the Earth's atmosphere, but in space. The space race was on!

The first American satellite, *Explorer 1,* was quickly sent into orbit on January 31, 1958. But President Dwight D. Eisenhower knew that satellites would not be enough. What America demanded was a man in space. That July, he formed the National Aeronautics and Space Administration, NASA. On December 17, 1958, the anniversary of the first Wright Brothers flight, NASA announced its first manned space project: Project Mercury, named after the winged messenger of the Roman gods. They were looking for a few good men to send into space: astronauts, sailors to the stars.

John Glenn was first in line.

CHAPTER FOUR

Becoming an Astronaut

John Glenn felt he was destined to be an astronaut. He had been training his body and mind for this challenge all his life. But how could he make sure he would be chosen?

Quite a few things were working against him. For one thing, there was his age. The age cutoff for Mercury astronauts was thirty-nine. Glenn was already thirty-seven, just under the wire. Then there was the problem of his incomplete education. NASA requirements specifically said that all astronauts had to have a college degree.

Finally, there was Glenn's size. Due to the tiny space inside the space capsule, no astronaut could be taller than five feet eleven inches—exactly Glenn's height—or heavier than 180 pounds. And after a few years at a

Navy desk job in Washington, DC, Glenn was weighing in at a hefty 208.

He set out to get in shape. With Tom Miller at his side, he jogged, lifted weights, swam, and dieted. In short order, he was down to 178 pounds.

The education requirement was harder to meet, though. Even after Glenn had transferred all the credits for the math and aerodynamics courses he'd taken over the years, Muskingum still would not grant him a degree. College administrators pointed out that he had not even lived in New Concord for the past seventeen years.

NASA winnowed the list down to eighty-eight candidates, all pilots who were used to putting their lives on the line every day. Glenn was still on the list. But not for long. Though he didn't know it at the time, his lack of a degree disqualified him. Later Glenn found out that his old commanding officer at the Naval Air Test Center had taken all of his records and qualifications over to NASA and argued his case. Thanks to that officer, Glenn was back in the running.

Now NASA was down to thirty-two candidates.

The lucky few were summoned to Lovelace Medical Clinic in Albuquerque, New Mexico, for medical tests. Glenn was told that he and his fellow candidates would be subject to the most complete medical tests ever given to any human being. Soon he decided this was no exaggeration.

For eight days Glenn and the others were pushed, prodded, and poked. He was turned upside down and practically inside out. He had blood tests, urine tests, bowel tests, eye and ear tests, tests that measured the contents of his stomach, and tests that probed the contents of his mind. "Wires and tubes dangled from us like tentacles from a jellyfish," Glenn said later. "Nobody wanted to tell us what some of the stranger tests were for."

Once, for instance, the doctors plunged a big needle attached to an electrical wire into the base of his thumb. Then they pressed a button. His hand started opening and closing automatically, faster and faster. What was the point of the test? Glenn never could figure it out.

Next, all candidates went over to Wright-Patterson Air Force Base for psychological testing. The object here was to see how much physical and mental stress they could endure before they became jittery—or totally freaked out.

First Glenn took the usual stress tests, like running on a treadmill to measure his heart rate and body temperature. Then came other, more unusual tests.

Becoming an Astronaut

They poured cold water in his ears to see whether he'd become dizzy and disoriented.

They strapped him to a chair that shook him like a human milkshake.

They placed him in a pressure chamber wearing an oxygen mask and a partial pressure suit and told him to breathe. Meanwhile, the air was gradually drawn out of the room. In-out, in-out, Glenn told himself, concentrating on each breath. His chest began to feel as though an elephant were sitting on it. But he forced himself to continue until the test was over.

One machine, called the "idiot box," tested reaction time. Glenn sat in front of an instrument panel with blinking lights and noisy beepers. He was told to push buttons and pull levers in a certain order to make the flashing, beeping, and buzzing stop. And then all the lights and beepers started going off at once! He tried to concentrate on the task without losing his cool. If he showed frustration, he knew he'd be out of the program.

One day, Glenn was led into an "isolation chamber"—a pitch-black, soundproof room—and left sitting in front of a desk. No one told him how long he'd be there. Glenn reached into the desk for a pad and into his pocket for a pencil. Then, although he couldn't see a thing, he started to write, keeping his place by tracking each line with his finger. While sitting there in the dark, he wrote lists of things to do.

Then he started writing poetry. As soon as he finished one line, he had to memorize it before he could move on to the next. The poem was about each person's responsibility to use his or her "unborn talents" to make the world a better place.

After three hours, the door finally opened and Glenn walked out into the bright light.

One test made Glenn glad he'd worked so hard to get into top physical shape. He had to puff into a tube that blew air under a column of mercury. The challenge was to keep the mercury level up through sheer lung power. Until then, the longest anyone had been able to hold the column up was 91 seconds.

Glenn blew slowly but steadily, willing himself to hold his breath as the clock ticked. Sixty seconds...90...120...130 seconds. He had beaten the record by 59 seconds!

Yet Glenn wasn't actually the champion. That honor went to Scott Carpenter, a handsome Navy Air Force pilot. Carpenter kept the mercury up for 171 seconds! Glenn looked at Carpenter with respect. That guy must be incredibly fit, he figured.

Finally the tests were completed and the applicants

went home to wait and worry. On April 6, Glenn got a call from Charles Donlan, the deputy director of NASA. He crossed his fingers.

"Congratulations," he heard Donlan say. "You've made it."

CHAPTER FIVE
The Star Sailors

There were seven astronauts in all: the Mercury Seven. They would be the pioneers of American manned space flight. John Glenn would get to know each of his fellow astronauts extremely well over the course of the next three years.

Alan Shepard was a crack Navy pilot from New Hampshire. His dry wit helped lighten many a tense situation. But Al didn't reveal much of himself to the others. It was hard to tell what was going on beneath that cool, calm exterior.

Like Glenn and Shepard, Gus Grissom had flown combat missions in Korea. He won the Flying Cross and Air Medal as an Air Force fighter pilot. Gus could be a real cutup. But he was all business when it counted.

Deke Slayton was an aeronautics engineer and a test

pilot in the Air Force. Stubborn and forceful, he never let go of a problem until he had found a solution.

Navy pilot Wally Shirra was probably the most outgoing and talkative of the Mercury Seven. His pride and joy was a bright yellow Austin Healy sports car.

Gordon Cooper, an Air Force major, was a born flyboy. At age eight, he had learned to fly. At sixteen, he completed his first solo. Now thirty-two, Gordo was the youngest in the group. He figured his comparative youth would give him more time and experience in the space program. "I'm planning on getting to the Moon," he would boast. "I think I'll get to Mars."

Athletic Scott Carpenter, Navy Air Force, was known as sensitive and articulate. As devoted to his wife Rene as Glenn was to Annie, Scott became Glenn's best friend in the program.

These were the seven star sailors. All of them were different, but at heart they were much alike. A more patriotic, competitive, confident group of daredevils could not be found anywhere. They all possessed the adventurous qualities—what journalist Tom Wolfe would call the "right stuff"—to go into space.

At their first joint meeting, Robert Gilreth, director of Project Mercury, warned the astronauts about the unknown dangers ahead. "If for any reason whatsoever you decide it's not for you," he told them, "you can go back to your respective services, no questions asked."

Not likely, Glenn thought. He was going to make it into space, no matter what!

The astronauts' first hurdle was the next day's press conference, planned to introduce the Mercury Seven to an eager nation. For most of them, the idea of talking to reporters was a whole lot scarier than blasting off in a rocket.

Blinding white television lights hit Glenn and the others as they walked out onto the stage at NASA's Washington headquarters. The room was jam-packed with reporters and photographers, all jostling each other for a good view. The astronauts sat down at a table on which was displayed a model of the Atlas rocket and a Mercury space capsule. They tried not to wince every time a flashbulb went off.

After the press kits were passed out to the reporters, NASA director T. Keith Glennan stood up. "It is my pleasure to introduce to you—and I consider it a very real honor, gentlemen—Malcolm S. Carpenter, Leroy G. Cooper, John H. Glenn Jr., Virgil I. Grissom, Walter M. Schirra Jr., Alan B. Shepard Jr., and Donald K. Slayton...the nation's Mercury astronauts." The room erupted in cheers and applause. These reporters are really excited, Glenn thought. They know something special is happening here.

Then the question-and-answer period started. Reporters wanted to know everything about these incredibly brave young men—where they grew up, what they believed in, why they thought going into space was important. They were interested in what *really* made the astronauts tick—and they knew their viewers and readers would be, too.

Most of the astronauts spoke very briefly. They were not used to talking about themselves in front of a camera. Only Glenn seemed comfortable answering all the personal questions. Someone asked him whether his wife and children had "had anything to say" about his decision. "My wife's attitude toward this has been the same as it has been all along through my flying," Glenn said. "If it is what I want to do, she is behind it, and the kids are, too, a hundred percent."

Another reporter asked about their religious beliefs. Glenn was happy to talk about his Presbyterian upbringing. "I was brought up believing that you are placed on earth...with certain talents and capabilities," he explained. "It is up to each of us to use those talents and capabilities as best you can."

It was clear that the reporters were hanging on his

every word. Glenn had shown that he could handle himself well in front of a national audience.

Finally a reporter raised the question the whole country was dying to ask. "Could I ask for a show of hands of how many are confident that they will come back from outer space?" he said.

The astronauts all looked at each other. Then, one by one, each raised his hand in the air. Sure, they were coming back. They'd survived years of perilous flying missions. What was a little old Atlas rocket compared to a dogfight with an enemy fighter plane?

John Glenn was so confident, he raised *both* hands in the air.

The next morning the Mercury astronauts woke up to discover they had become national heroes. Newspapers across the country praised their bravery and patriotism. These courageous men, the *New York Times* raved, "spoke of 'duty' and 'faith' and 'country' like pioneers."

It looked as if the astronauts were going to be overwhelmed by media attention. Obviously they didn't have the time to fend off hundreds of snoopy reporters. So they decided to all band together and sign a deal with just one news organization—*Life* magazine. Only *Life,* it was agreed, would be permitted a glimpse into the homes and lives of Mercury astronauts. In return, each astronaut would receive $24,000 a year for three years. That was a great deal more money than any of them had ever made for one year in the military.

About three weeks later, they all went to Cape Canaveral, Florida, to watch the launch of an Atlas rocket. The Atlas was America's first intercontinental ballistic missile (ICBM), powered by lox and RP-1 kerosene. If all went well, some of the astronauts would someday sit in a space capsule that would ride an Atlas rocket into orbit around the earth.

Although it had been in development since the mid-1950s, the Atlas still had a few glitches. Quite a few, in fact.

Glenn watched as the engines ignited and the mighty silver rocket rose in a burst of yellow-white flame and smoke. Up, up it roared into the sky—and then it exploded. The astronauts watched in silence as blackened shards of metal tumbled into the Atlantic Ocean.

"Well, I'm glad they got that out of the way," Al Shepard joked.

Glenn and the others looked at each other in dismay. Would they ever make it into space?

CHAPTER SIX

Mean Machines

Now the real training began. For the next two years, while NASA engineers worked furiously to build a better and safer rocket, the astronauts got ready for space flight.

The goal of Mercury training was not just to prepare the seven men for anything they might encounter during their missions. It was to *over*prepare them. The astronauts had to know exactly how space flight would feel and sound and look—long before one of them was locked into a small metal container and blasted into the outer void. Alone.

The Mercury Seven not only faced a tough training schedule, but they also had to prove the importance of their roles in the space program. Some of the other test pilots joked that astronauts weren't real pilots at all. They were helpless robots, controlled by a computer back on Earth. After all, the test pilots pointed out, the first "astronauts" to make the trip into space would not be men at all—but monkeys! Hey, the famous Mercury Seven were really no better than "Spam in a can!"

Glenn, Grissom, Shepard, Cooper, Carpenter, Slayton, and Shirra were determined to prove all those envious test pilots wrong. Without their expert skills, they insisted, the Mercury program would fail. Only astronauts could make tough decisions on the spot if anything went wrong. Only pilots could guide a disabled spacecraft back to Earth again.

Throughout their training, the astronauts pushed for a more active role in the space flight. They wanted a hand controller that would let them guide the spacecraft if they needed to. They wanted a hatch on the spacecraft they could open themselves. But one of their demands seemed more important than all the rest.

They needed a window! The Mercury Seven were going to be the first human beings to venture into the immense universe beyond Earth—and there would be no way for them to see it! The NASA engineers had actually designed the Mercury capsule without a window. Sure, they would have a periscope, but that would give them a very limited view of the outside world. It was no substitute for the real thing.

The astronauts put their foot down. The spacecraft has to have a window, they told NASA.

A window will add too much weight, the design team argued.

No window, no mission, the Mercury Seven shot back.

So the designers went back to work. Finally the astronauts got their window.

For the next three years, the Mercury Seven worked harder than they had ever worked in their lives. First they had to educate themselves in space science. Since they would need to understand the mathematics of flight, they had to study physics. And astronomy, so they could plot their course by the stars. And physiology, so they would understand how their bodies reacted to weightlessness and the force of gravity. Becoming an astronaut, they soon discovered, was like getting a graduate degree in advanced science!

Then there was the physical training. The goal of the training was to imitate—or *simulate*—conditions within the capsule. For instance, astronauts had to get used to the high G forces of takeoff and reentry. A "G" is the unit that measures gravitational force. The pressure of one G is equal to the force of gravity on Earth.

To simulate G forces, the astronauts trained in a

centrifuge machine—called the Big Wheel—attached to a 50-foot arm. At the end of the arm was a cab designed to look like the inside of a Mercury capsule.

Dressed in a pressure suit, the astronaut was strapped into a seat molded to the shape of his body. The centrifuge whirled the arm around, faster and faster. As it accelerated, he would be pressed back against the seat. The forces would climb to three, then five, then eight Gs, equal to the pressure he would feel when the rocket shot up to an altitude of 65 miles. When the spacecraft went into actual orbit, the G forces would disappear and the astronaut would become weightless. Afterwards, when the capsule reentered the atmosphere, the pressure would rise again.

Throughout the whole exercise, the astronauts were instructed to talk into their headsets, as if they were in actual flight. Fighting the pressure, they had to lift their arms to push buttons and pull levers on the instrument panel. They learned to perform the necessary tasks with minimum effort. And they got used to the Big Wheel, though training in it was never comfortable.

How many Gs could the human body stand? To find out, John Glenn and two others were chosen as human guinea pigs. This time, to reduce the pressure, Glenn lay down almost flat in his molded seat. He tested his reactions as the pressure gauge rose steadily.

8 Gs...9 Gs...10 Gs. Now Glenn could no longer raise his arms.

11 Gs...12 Gs. He kept tensing his muscles to keep the blood moving.

13 Gs...14 Gs. He started to grunt. This helped his heart pump the blood throughout the body. Otherwise, it would all pool in the middle.

15 Gs...16 Gs. Now he had to fight to remain conscious. The seconds ticked by—and then the centrifuge slowed down. Glenn was dizzy, but okay.

NASA doctors decided that sixteen Gs was about as much as the human body could withstand. That was the equivalent of 2,800 pounds of push against the body!

Another potential problem was weightlessness. How would the human body react when it was no longer subject to the pull of gravity? No one knew—but the possibilities were frightening. Would eyes lose their shape? Would the throat be able to swallow? Would astronauts go blind, or choke on their food?

NASA engineers had no way to simulate zero-G for a long period of time. The best they could offer Glenn and the others was a few precious seconds of weightlessness—in parabolic flight. (A parabola is a U-shaped curve.)

The engineers had the astronauts travel as passengers in the back of training planes. After the pilot took the plane up to 40,000 feet, he dived down quickly and then soared up again, in one long, smooth arc. During the ride up, the gravity of the climb balanced the pull of Earth's gravity—and the astronaut passengers were weightless for as long as sixty seconds.

Since they were strapped in, they couldn't float around inside the airplane. But they could practice pushing buttons, eating, and drinking in zero-G. The astronauts experimented with eating pureed beef and drinking tomato or orange juice. Al Shepard liked to squirt the juice right into his mouth. Gus Grissom, though, got a kick out of spraying juice into the cabin—and then watching the big orange bubbles float around in front of his nose.

Another top priority for the astronauts was to learn to handle an orbiting spacecraft that was tumbling out of control. As experienced pilots, all the astronauts knew that the position of a craft in space is called its "attitude." Attitude is determined by three movements: pitch, roll, and yaw. Pitch is the movement around the side-to-side axis of the spacecraft. Roll is the movement around the front-to-back axis. And yaw is the movement around its vertical axis.

Ordinarily, an automatic pilot system controlled the capsule. But if the automatic pilot failed, then the *real* pilot could step in and guide the capsule by hand.

Just one control stick directed all three movements, pitch, roll, and yaw. Moving the stick back and forth controlled its up-and-down motion (pitch). Moving it right or left controlled its sideways turn (roll). And rotating it controlled its side-to-side motion (yaw).

To practice, the astronauts were strapped into a nasty machine known as MASTIF—Multi-Axis Space Training Inertial Facility. It consisted of three round metal frameworks, set one inside another. The outside framework pitched, the middle framework rolled, and the inner framework yawed. The astronauts sat inside, Gus Grissom wrote later, "spinning violently in three different directions at once—head over heels, round and round as if you were on a merry-go-round, and sideways as if your arms and legs were tied to the spokes of a wheel." It was up to the astronaut to swivel the control stick until all the twisting and rolling stopped. Then he would stumble out—and lie down on a cot until the dizziness went away!

So far, their training had prepared the astronauts to cope with the challenges of space flight: high G forces, weightlessness, and an out-of-control spacecraft. Now their pretend spacecraft was falling back to Earth—and they had to prepare for a landing. What should they do?

Each mission would be provided with a standard survival kit, which included shark repellent, a raft, a dye marker, sunglasses, and zinc oxide for sunburn. If the capsule splashed down in the ocean, as it was supposed to, then these items would help keep the astronaut safe until a helicopter arrived to pick him up.

Out in the Gulf of Mexico, the astronauts practiced inflating their rafts and climbing out of a bobbing capsule with their pressure suits on. At one point, the waves were so high that Glenn's raft turned over and he tumbled into the water. Another time, Deke Slayton took his helmet off before leaving his capsule. Seawater poured down his neck into his suit—and he almost drowned before he could reach his life raft. As a result, NASA engineers went back and designed a new waterproof neck seal.

So much for a water landing. But what if the spacecraft went off course and came down on solid ground instead?

Just in case, the astronauts took a survival class out in the hot, dry Nevada desert. There Glenn and the others learned how to turn their parachute into a sun-blocking poncho. To test the results of dehydration, they didn't drink any water for twenty-four hours. As Glenn lay under the shade of a cactus at the end of the day, he was so weak he could barely raise his hand.

One instructor showed them how to suck the venom

out of a snakebite wound. To prove the venom wasn't poisonous if swallowed, he poured some water moccasin venom into a glass—and gulped it down!

Glenn grimaced. He'd do his best to stay away from the desert—and snakes!

Meanwhile, the astronauts continued to attend one rocket launch after another. On July 29, 1960, they went to a test flight of the final model of the Atlas missile. The Atlas was the missile that would eventually propel the Mercury capsule into orbit. (A smaller rocket, the Redstone, would propel the earlier suborbital flights.) Unfortunately, the Atlas had a failure rate of 45 percent. Discouraged, the public was beginning to grumble about the cost of the space program. NASA badly needed a success.

Hundreds of people—astronauts, Congressmen, and other VIPs—were invited to watch the launch from a nearby grandstand. On schedule, the mammoth missile fired in a burst of orange flame and rose slowly from the launch pad.

Spectators craned their necks to watch the rocket soar up into the clouds and disappear from view. Then, far off, came the sound of an explosion.

Another bust. With a sinking heart, Glenn realized that this latest failure would delay the first Mercury launch by months.

He tried to reassure his family, though. "They'll go back to the drawing board and get it fixed," he said.

Meanwhile, many Americans were concerned about the success of the Soviet space program. In 1957, Russians sent a dog into orbit around the Earth. In September 1959, they sent a probe to the Moon. NASA, on the other hand, couldn't seem to get a rocket off the ground without having it explode.

Four months later, the VIPs came back for another launch, this time of a Redstone rocket. The Redstone had been much more successful than the Atlas, and everyone expected a smooth liftoff. The visitors settled back to watch a good show.

"Three...two...one! We have ignition!"

A blast of red and orange shot out of the tail of the rocket. The Redstone rose up about four inches off the launch pad—and then settled back down again. "It was like watching the fizzle of some gigantic Roman candle at a Fourth of July celebration," Glenn said later.

A second later he heard a loud *pop!* as the escape tower on top of the capsule shot off. It drifted down gently under a parachute. It was another total disaster for NASA. Things were definitely not looking good.

All these public failures just made the astronauts more determined to make their contribution to the Mercury program a success.

The biggest question on their minds was: Who would make the first flight? The first man in space would be a world hero, the one astronaut guaranteed to go down in the history books. Naturally each one of these super-dedicated, super-achieving, super-competitive pilots wanted to be that man. "Anyone who doesn't *want* to be first doesn't belong in this program," Glenn admitted at a press conference.

Secretly, Glenn believed he was the best qualified to go. He was sure NASA would pick him.

But Project Mercury chief Bob Gilruth surprised everyone. In fall 1960, he called the astronauts to a meeting and asked for a vote. "If you can't make the first flight yourself," he said, "who do you think should make it?"

Glenn was outraged. The Mercury program was supposed to be all about skill—not popularity!

After the astronauts had voted by secret ballot, Gilruth brought them all together again. NASA had made a decision, he said. The first man in space would be...Alan Shepard!

Glenn was stunned. He felt he'd missed his shot at immortality.

Gilruth continued. Gus Grissom and John Glenn would fly second or third, he announced. Glenn would be Shepard's backup for the first flight. If anything happened to Al, John would take his place.

Being chosen backup was no consolation, Glenn thought. To make matters worse, the choice for the first flight had to remain a secret. The public assumed that John Glenn was the favorite. For the next few months, Glenn would have to pretend he still had a chance.

Glenn tried to swallow his disappointment and get back to work. The team came first, he told himself.

Now events moved rapidly ahead. On January 31, 1961, a Redstone rocket blasted off successfully with a male chimpanzee named Ham onboard. NASA had chosen a chimpanzee to make the test flight because chimpanzees were closer to humans, both physically and mentally, than were any other animals.

The chimp flight was far from perfect, though. Ham was subjected to seven Gs on the way up—and more than fifteen on the way down! That grin he flashed at the cameras when he was pulled from the water wasn't a smile of happiness. It was a grimace of fear.

But he did come down, and he was alive. If a chimp could survive a space flight, so could Al Shepard.

The team threw itself into a frenzy of preparation. Shepard was scheduled to go up in a suborbital flight on March 24. But then the engineers decided the Redstone needed one more test, and more time passed…

The delay was costly. On April 12, 1961, a Soviet cosmonaut named Yuri Gagarin completed one full orbit around the Earth.

The Russians had won the race to send a man into space!

CHAPTER SEVEN

Into the Space Age

The news was devastating. Not only the Mercury astronauts, but all Americans felt disappointment. When a reporter asked Glenn for his reaction, he tried to sound realistic but upbeat. "Well, they just beat the pants off us, that's all, and there's no use kidding ourselves about that," he said. "But now that that space age has begun, there's going to be plenty of work for everybody."

Luckily, no one had a chance to dwell on the missed opportunity. Al Shepard's real launch date was coming up, and fast.

Early on the morning of May 5, 1961, Glenn woke up with Shepard in the crew quarters at Cape Canaveral. As mission backup, Glenn rode the elevator up the side of the Redstone rocket to give the capsule one last check before launch. Before he finished, he left a sign

in the tiny space: "No Handball Playing in This Area."
He was sure Al would get a chuckle out of it.

Shortly after 5:00 A.M., Glenn helped squeeze Al feet-
first into his capsule, *Freedom 7*. Then Glenn went back
to Mercury Control Center to help oversee the countdown. Four times the launch was put on hold, and four
times the clock started again. Hours slipped by.

Through his earphones, Glenn heard Shepard make
an urgent request. He had to urinate—immediately—
and didn't know what to do. The suborbital flight was
short, only fifteen minutes, and no one had bothered
to plan for a rest stop on the spacecraft.

"Do it in your suit," Glenn was forced to say.

At T minus 2 minutes and 40 seconds, the clock
stopped again. This time engineers were worried about
pressure on the liquid oxygen. Shepard got back on the
mike. "I'm cooler than you are," Al said. Glenn could
hear the impatience in his voice. "Why don't you fix
your little problem and light this candle?"

The countdown resumed.

At 9:34 A.M., the rockets fired. The Redstone rocket
lifted into the air. "Roger, liftoff and the clock is
started," Shepard announced.

In its historic fifteen-minute flight, *Freedom 7* soared
to an altitude of 115,696 miles above Earth. After just

a few minutes of weightlessness, Shepard rode the capsule back down to Earth. *Freedom 7* splashed into the Atlantic Ocean just 302 miles from Cape Canaveral. It was a near-perfect mission.

Tense and excited, Americans watched every suspenseful moment on TV, anxiously sweating it out along with the team at Mission Control. In the White House, President John F. Kennedy and his wife Jackie kept their eyes glued to the black-and-white TV in the Oval Office. After Shepard was located at sea and brought aboard a waiting aircraft carrier, Kennedy phoned to offer his congratulations.

From coast to coast, America celebrated. Finally, as Glenn wrote later, "the United States had entered the space age."

Two weeks later, on May 25, Kennedy delivered an important speech to Congress. "Now is the time to take longer strides," he declared, "time for a great new American enterprise.... I believe this nation should commit itself to achieving the goal, before this decade is out, of landing a man on the moon and returning him safely to Earth." The audience exploded in cheers. Everyone at NASA breathed a sigh of relief. Now they could be sure that the program for which they had worked so long and hard would continue.

Glenn still hoped he would be chosen to make the second flight. But he was passed by once more, this time in favor of Gus Grissom. Again Glenn had to grit his teeth and pretend it didn't matter. But it did.

Gus went up in Mercury's second suborbital flight on July 19, 1961. The night before launch, he and Glenn figured out a solution to that little bathroom problem. They glued some rubber tubing onto a plastic bag that would be taped to the astronaut's leg. The gimmick worked.

Only this time the mission did not go exactly according to plan. After the capsule, *Liberty Bell 7,* fell into the ocean, the hatch blew off and water started pouring in. Quickly Grissom pulled off his helmet and hoisted himself over the edge of the capsule and into the frigid ocean. In spite of the seal, water rushed into his neck hole, and the space suit grew heavy and water-logged. Grissom had to paddle hard to keep his head above the waves.

He heard the *whirr* of a helicopter hovering above. Grissom waved his arm. But strangely, no one threw down a life belt! "Well," Grissom thought to himself, "you've gone through the whole flight, and now you're going to sink right here in front of all these people."

Finally another helicopter came in and tossed him a sling. Exhausted, Grissom hung on as they hauled him up into the copter. But *Liberty Bell 7* sank too fast to be recovered. His spacecraft was gone. It would be the only Mercury capsule lost at sea.

Aboard the carrier, an officer handed Grissom his helmet. "For your information," the officer said, "we found it floating next to a ten-foot shark."

The team was disappointed that *Liberty Bell 7* was lost, but happy that Gus was okay and the overall mission a success. They began to prepare for another suborbital flight.

Then came more unwelcome news. On August 6, the Soviets sent another cosmonaut into orbit. Gherman Titov circled the earth an incredible total of seventeen times over a twenty-five-hour period.

NASA scrambled for a response. Clearly they couldn't just shoot another astronaut up into the air and down again. This time, the spacecraft would have travel further and longer. This time, it would have to orbit.

Glenn knew he was supposedly next in line. Still, he worried whether he would be chosen. He had just turned forty years old, after all. Would NASA decide that he was too old to fly?

NASA made its preparations. The Redstone rocket was too small; it did not have enough thrust—only 76,000 pounds—to insert a capsule into orbit. For the first orbital flight, the mighty Atlas missile, with its

360,000 pounds of thrust, would be used instead. Only the Atlas could boost the capsule up to the extraordinary speed of 18,000 miles per hour.

Over the next few months, the Atlas was tested again and again. On September 13, it successfully propelled a dummy astronaut into one orbit of the Earth. Then, on November 29, came the turn of another chimp, named Enos. He got so excited that he ripped out all the biosensors that tracked his heartbeat, blood pressure, and pulse. Still, Enos made it back safely and even had his own news conference.

Who was going to follow the chimp into orbit? one of the reporters wanted to know.

"John Glenn will make the next flight," Bob Gilruth answered. "Scott Carpenter will be his backup."

Finally, Glenn was going into space.

CHAPTER EIGHT
Waiting Game

ASA hoped to schedule the first orbital flight before Christmas. That gave Glenn less than a month to get ready.

One of his first tasks was to decide on a name for his capsule. He turned the job over to his children. Together, Dave and Lyn wrote up a list of possibilities: Columbia, Endeavor, America, Magellan, We, Hope. Their first choice, though, was Friendship.

Perfect, Glenn thought. *Friendship* 7 it would be. He asked the NASA artist to paint the name on the side of the capsule in script letters, right next to the picture of an American flag.

At first Glenn kept to his regular routine, training in the simulator and running two miles each day on the sand. He and Scott Carpenter sometimes drove into nearby Cocoa Beach to have dinner at a Polynesian restaurant. But as the excitement grew, Glenn began to be trailed by groups of reporters. They even followed him to church on Sundays. Eventually he decided to go into isolation. He felt he needed complete concentration for the task ahead.

John and Scott moved into the crew quarters at Hangar S on the Cape. Staying away from other people, Glenn hoped, would keep him from catching the flu or a winter cold. The owner of a nearby motel, Henri Landwirth, sent them regular "care packages" of delicious food. Glenn especially loved the shrimp with hot sauce and black bread.

Scott came and went, but John stayed close to base. Friends started to send him mock get-well cards. "Sorry to hear about your long confinement," one read.

One night Henri called to invite him to his home for dinner. Why not? Glenn thought. He hadn't been off the base for weeks. He looked forward to a relaxed evening with good food.

The evening was a success, but the next morning Henri called again. "I hope you've had the mumps," he said, opening the conversation. His daughter, he reported, had just come down with them.

The mumps! No, Glenn never had had them. A week later, he woke up with a sore neck and began to panic. Surely, it couldn't be... Luckily, it turned out that Glenn had merely strained his neck muscles the day before.

As December 20 neared, NASA decided to scrap the pre-Christmas launch. A new date of January 16 was set, and Glenn went home to Arlington, Virginia, for the holidays.

One afternoon, John, Annie, and the kids went to snowy Great Falls, Virginia, for a winter cookout. As they sat on the rocks and listened to the sound of the falling water, fifteen-year-old Lyn raised a subject they had all been thinking about. "What kinds of things could happen to you, Dad?"

Glenn knew she was talking about a possible accident, or even death. All the astronauts knew that there were risks, he told his family. But everyone on Project Mercury had worked hard to minimize them.

"If I believed something was likely to happen," he told Lyn and Dave, "I wouldn't want to go, and NASA wouldn't send me in the first place. But if anything did happen to go wrong, I don't want you to blame anybody, okay? Not NASA, not anybody. I'm doing something I really want to do because it's important for our whole country. And it's something we should keep doing, so don't let anybody tell you we should stop trying to get into space."

After the first of the year, the flight was delayed again

and again because of bad weather. January 16 came and went, and a new date of January 23 was set—and then canceled. On January 27, Glenn spent six hours in the capsule waiting for liftoff. It never came. Tired and discouraged, he went back to Hangar S.

There he was met by a group of NASA officials. Could he give Annie a call? they asked. The matter was urgent.

Annie, Glenn knew, was under siege back in Arlington. Reporters were camped out on her front lawn, waiting for a glimpse of the astronaut's brave wife and children. Luckily, the exclusive *Life* contract protected her from actually having to talk with anyone but *Life* reporter Loudon Wainwright. Annie's stutter was still quite bad, and the thought of having to give a press conference made her very nervous.

So John called Annie and she explained the situation. Vice-president Lyndon B. Johnson was parked in a limousine just a block away from the house, waiting to invade with a slew of television reporters. He wanted to console Annie for the delayed flight. The interview was to be broadcast on national TV. Not only that, but Johnson had also demanded that *Life* reporter Wainwright leave the house so the other reporters could get their chance.

She didn't want to meet with Johnson, Annie told her husband. It had been a very long day and she had a headache.

Glenn promptly came to her rescue. "Look, if you don't want the vice-president or the TV networks or anybody else to come into the house, then that's it as far as I'm concerned. They are not coming in—and I will back you up all the way, one hundred percent!"

The NASA officials were very unhappy. A mere astronaut and his wife had dared to defy the Vice President of the United States! One official told Glenn to his face that if he didn't cooperate, he could be replaced. When he heard the threat, Glenn said afterward, he "saw red."

Fine, Glenn said deliberately. NASA could go ahead and dismiss him and announce it on national TV. Then Glenn could have his own press conference and tell *his* side of the story. In the meantime, he said, he had to go take a shower.

Glenn walked off down the hall. He never heard another word about the incident.

The launch date was pushed forward again. President Kennedy invited Glenn to come to the White House to explain the mission to him. With the help of models and blueprints, Glenn took the fascinated president through the flight, step by step.

By now, everyone was jittery. One of the most impatient was Glenn's friend Henri Landwirth. He had baked the world's largest cake—900 pounds!—to celebrate the flight. He had stored the cake, which looked just like *Friendship 7*, in an air-conditioned truck to keep it from spoiling.

Finally the next launch date dawned—February 20. Glenn woke at 1:30 A.M., suited up, and was strapped into the capsule couch. The procedure was extremely familiar by now—he'd been through it four times before.

The countdown began, then stopped. It looked as if the clouds were thinning off the Cape. Glenn took advantage of the delay to call his family. They were watching the launch on television back in Arlington.

"Hey, honey," Glenn said to Annie as he had so many times before. "Don't be scared. Remember, I'm just going down to the corner store to get a pack of gum."

"Don't be long," she said, trying to sound upbeat.

"I'll talk to you after I land this afternoon," he promised her. The countdown started again.

Outside the capsule, the clouds scattered. It was turning into a beautiful day, with a brilliant blue sky. The clock clicked steadily forward.

At 9:47 A.M., the count reached zero.

"Ignition!" called the countdown person in Mission Control.

Glenn could feel a deep rumble as the engines started up far beneath him. The Atlas belched flame and smoke.

"Liftoff!" the voice cried again.

Glenn felt a very definite sensation of "up and away." This, then, was it. The moment he had been waiting for...

Over the headset came Scott Carpenter's muffled message: "Godspeed, John Glenn."

CHAPTER NINE

The Mission

Glenn glanced at the mission clock in the cockpit. "The clock is operating," he said. "We're underway!"

The great rocket rose up, gradually gathering speed. At thirteen seconds he could feel the vibrations starting as the Atlas forced its way through the air. "Little bumpy about here," he reported.

The G forces began to build. *2 Gs...3 Gs...4 Gs.* Glenn was forced back into his seat. After all those hours on the centrifuge, the pressure felt very familiar. Yet, he noticed, the real thing was a lot gentler than the Big Wheel!

Now the Atlas was pushing through the heavy atmosphere at a thousand pounds per square foot. This was "max Q," maximum aerodynamic pressure. If the rocket were defective, this was the moment it would explode...

4 Gs...5 Gs.

Suddenly, at 1 minute 16 seconds, the air thinned and the flight smoothed out. "Roger, you're through max," he heard Al Shepard say over the headset.

Whew, Glenn thought. He had passed through the first danger zones—and he was supersonic!

6 Gs. At 2 minutes 9 seconds, the booster engines that had thrust the Atlas off the launch pad switched off and fell away. Abruptly, the pressure dropped.

Now the rocket was free of the lower atmosphere. "Sky looking very dark outside," Glenn reported to Mission Control. The Atlas sustainer engines kept pushing the capsule higher and faster, consuming fuel at one ton per second. The pressure started to build again, rising all the way up to 6 Gs.

Glenn read off the fuel, oxygen, cabin pressure, and battery measurements from the dials on the instrument panel. Everything was fine.

"Cape is go and I am go. Capsule is in good shape," he reported.

"Roger. Twenty seconds to SECO," said Shepard. At Sustainer Engine Cutoff, the Atlas rocket engine would insert the capsule into orbit. The bolts that held the Atlas and the capsule together unclamped, and rockets fired to push them apart. The Atlas was flung out into space.

Abruptly, Glenn dropped into zero-G. He was weightless!

Five minutes after liftoff, *Friendship 7* was in orbit, 100 miles above the earth, circling it at 25,730 feet per second.

"Zero-G and I feel fine!" Glenn said exultantly. "Capsule is turning around." The capsule was facing blunt end forward, so that Glenn would be traveling backward throughout the voyage. It was a lot like sitting backward on a speeding train, with the landscape rolling by him in reverse.

Through the window, he could see the curved Earth far below, wrapped in its thin, filmy atmosphere. "Oh," he exclaimed. "That view is tremendous!" The Atlas tumbled away from the capsule, shining in the light of the sun.

Thus far, it had been a perfect mission. From Mission Control, Shepard said, "You have a go, at least seven orbits."

Seven orbits! It was more than Glenn had hoped for.

Glenn was going east, over the Atlantic Ocean. Far below him, the route was lined with capsule communications (capcom) stations that stretched around the globe: Bermuda; the Canary Islands; Kano, Nigeria; Zanzibar; a ship out on the Indian Ocean; Muchea, Australia; Woomera, Australia; Canton Island in the

Pacific; Guaymas; California; Cape Canaveral. If all went well, Glenn would never be out of communication with the ground for more than a few minutes in the whole flight.

Most of the voyage would be spent running through a checklist of tasks—medical experiments, systems tests, instrument reports. The whole flight plan was typed on a tiny scroll of paper that he unrolled item by item.

"This is *Friendship Seven,*" he told Gus Grissom, the capcom at the Bermuda station. "Working just like clockwork on the control check, and it went through just about like the procedures trainer runs."

Next, Glenn reached in to get his camera from the equipment kit located next to his right arm. The first item to float out was a little gray, felt-toy mouse with pink ears. Glenn grinned. He knew immediately that Al Shepard had left it as a joke. They both loved a popular comedy routine about poor mice that were sent into space in rocket nose cones.

The mouse was fastened to the pouch by a long string that kept it from floating away. So was the camera, an automatic 35 mm Glenn had picked out himself. NASA engineers had made alterations so someone wearing thick gloves could operate it. He snapped pictures of clouds over the Atlantic and dust storms over the Sahara Desert.

Above Zanzibar, Glenn exercised with a bungee cord attached under the instrument panel. Sure enough, his pulse rate went up, just as it did when he worked out back on earth. Apparently, weightlessness made no difference in ordinary body reactions.

So he tried some other tests. He read the eye chart and discovered that his vision was normal. Eyeballs did not change shape in zero-G after all. He moved his head from side to side and felt no dizziness. Altogether, weightlessness was a lot more pleasant than some of the tests he'd endured during his training!

Forty minutes into the flight came his first real treat—a sunset. To prepare for it, Glenn placed red filters over the lights on the instrument panel and turned on tiny flashlights at the end of his fingers. This way, the light inside the capsule would not interfere with the night lights outside.

He planned to watch the sunset through a photometer, which was equipped with a filter to protect his eyes. As the sun sank over the western horizon of Earth, the band of brilliant light on the horizon changed from white to orange, then burst into red, purple, and bright blue before finally fading away into black. It was more spectacular than a hundred fireworks displays. Glenn snapped another picture.

"The sunset was beautiful," Glenn told the capcom stationed on a ship out in the middle of the Indian Ocean. "I still have a brilliant blue band clear across the horizon almost covering my whole window…the sky above is absolutely black…I can see stars, though, up above." *Friendship 7* was zooming so fast around the earth that the whole show lasted only five or six minutes.

He had expected that here above the atmosphere, the stars would look exceptionally bright. But they looked no different than they would on a clear night in the desert. The thick glass of the window, it seemed, acted like an atmospheric filter—it made stars appear fuzzy and indistinct. Still, he could recognize some of his favorite constellations, such as Orion and the Pleiades. As he had hoped, he was able to use Orion to maintain attitude.

As Glenn flew over Australia, he recognized Gordon Cooper's voice through his earphones. "How are you doing, Gordo?" he greeted him. "We're doing real fine up here. Everything is going very well. Over."

"John, you sound good," Cooper replied.

Glenn gave him the systems report, then added, "That sure was a short day."

Cooper couldn't quite hear him. "Say again, *Friendship Seven.*"

"That was about the shortest day I've ever run in to," Glenn repeated.

"Kinda passes rapidly, huh?"

"Yes sir."

Cooper suggested that Glenn keep his eyes open for lights on the ground. Glenn peered out into the darkness beneath him. Sure enough, he spied thousands of twinkling lights.

"Just to my right I can see a big pattern of lights apparently right on the coast. I can see the outline of a town and a very bright light just to the south of it."

"Perth and Rockingham, you're seeing there," Cooper explained. Even though it was the middle of the night, Australians had switched on every light in their homes and businesses to welcome the space traveler circling above them.

Glenn was appreciative. "The lights show up very well and thank everybody for turning them on, will you?"

It was time for his first and only meal of the journey— applesauce. He placed the toothpaste tube in midair while he raised the visor on his helmet. Then he screwed on the straw and squeezed the applesauce into his mouth. Not a drop was lost.

His first sunrise came right in the middle of the Pacific Ocean, just thirty-five minutes after sunset.

Because he was riding into it, he couldn't see the sunrise directly, but had to view it backwards through the periscope. "The brilliant blue horizon coming up behind me; approaching sunrise," he reported.

"Roger, *Friendship Seven.* You are very lucky."

"You're right. Man, this is beautiful."

And then, he saw them, a million little swirling lights, just outside the capsule window.

Glenn drew his breath in sharply. What in the world could they be?

CHAPTER TEN

Flying-by-Wire

This is *Friendship Seven,*" Glenn said. "I'll try to describe what I'm in here. I am in a big mass of some very small particles that are brilliantly lit up. I never saw anything like it. They're coming by the capsule. They look like little stars."

"Roger, *Friendship Seven,*" Canton Island capcom said. "Can you hear any impact with the capsule?"

"Negative," Glenn replied. "They're very slow. They're going at the same speed I am approximately. There are literally thousands of them."

He was fascinated by the particles. They looked like fireflies dancing on a summer night. They couldn't actually be living things, though, not out here, where there was no air to breathe. Alien fireflies, then? Not likely.

Or maybe they were more like tiny snowflakes in a blizzard. Could they be ice particles that had sprayed out of the control nozzle? It didn't look that way. True, they were traveling at about the same speed as he was. But they were swirling all around him and into the distance. How could they be coming from the capsule?

Whatever they were, they sure were beautiful.

Strangely, Glenn had difficulty getting anyone on the ground to pay attention to the lights. All the capcom at Guaymas wanted to know about were the instrument readings.

Glenn tried to load his camera with a second roll of film. But the film wasn't tethered to the equipment pouch. When he reached for it, his hand knocked into it. The roll lodged behind the instrument panel and he couldn't retrieve it. This is frustrating, Glenn thought. In space, nothing stays put!

As the sun got brighter, the particles faded away, their mystery still unsolved. Suddenly, though, they didn't matter any more. Glenn had something more urgent to worry about.

Without warning, the capsule yawed to the right. To correct the movement, the right-hand thruster outside the capsule fired off a blast of hydrogen and pushed the capsule back to the left. Then it drifted to the right again. Something was way out of whack. Back and forth the *Friendship 7* bounced, first to the right, then to the left. Obviously the automatic pilot control system was going haywire.

Glenn knew what he had to do. He took hold of the manual control stick. "I'm going fly-by-wire," he told Wally Schirra, the California capcom. The fly-by-wire system would let him direct the capsule's attitude by hand.

The real worry, Glenn knew, was not that the capsule would drift off course. The course had been set by computer before *Friendship 7* ever left Cape Canaveral. The danger was that the thrusters would use up their supply of hydrogen fuel trying to correct the yaw. Then he wouldn't have enough fuel to direct the capsule at reentry. *Friendship 7* had to enter the atmosphere at exactly the right angle, with its round, blunt end facing down. If the angle was off by a thousandth of a degree...

Well, there was no use thinking about it now.

So as he crossed the continental United States, Glenn continued to fly-by-wire. Over the Cape, Al Shepard told him to stand by for President Kennedy. Glenn was eager to speak to the president. But he never came on. Some problem with the radio hookup, perhaps.

"Having no trouble controlling," Glenn told Shepard. "Very smooth and easy, controls very nicely."

Now he was beginning his second orbit. He kept testing the automatic pilot system to see if it was working. But by the time he contacted the ship out in the middle of the Atlantic, the automatic steering was still fouled up. "My troubles in yaw appear to have largely reversed," he reported. "At one time I had no left low thrust in yaw. Now that one is working and I now have no right thrust in yaw."

He went back to manual control, this time swinging the capsule around 180 degrees. For the first time during the flight, he was facing forward. "I like this attitude very much, so you can see where you're going," Glenn told the capcom ship in the Atlantic.

He swung the capsule back to orbit attitude again. Now he could see lightning above the Atlantic Ocean, little sparks glittering inside the clouds.

Glenn liked flying manually. It put him in control, like a real pilot, and it proved to the guys back at NASA that it was important to have a human in the spacecraft. Without him, the *Friendship 7* would never make it back to Earth.

His second sunset blazed forth while he was over Africa. He gave his thirty-minute status report. His head movement still caused no nausea, he said. He had "no trouble reading the charts," he told them, "no problem with astigmatism at all. I'm having no trouble holding attitudes either. I'm still on fly-by-wire."

The capcom in the Indian Ocean ship forwarded him a message from Mission Control to keep his landing bag switch in the off position.

That's strange, Glenn thought. Why are they worrying about the landing bag now? The landing bag was the cushion that opened up just before splashdown. He glanced at the switch. Sure enough, it was off.

Soon it became obvious that more than his yaw was out of order. Now he started having problems with the automatic pitch and roll, too. Funny, he thought. The instrument panel told him that everything was fine. "My attitudes are not matching what I see out the window," he informed the capcom.

It was a good thing Glenn had spent so much time in MASTIF during training. Now he was having to orient the capsule using the control stick in all three positions—pitch, roll, and yaw—just as he had been trained to do.

From the Muchea station, Gordo Cooper asked again, "Will you confirm that landing bag switch is in off position? Over."

"That is affirmative."

"You haven't had any banging noises or anything of this type at higher rates?"

"Negative." Why this sudden interest in the landing bag? Glenn wondered.

Come dawn, he spied another swarm of mysterious lights. "They're all over the sky," he reported. "Way out I can see them, as far as I can see in each direction."

Again, he couldn't drum up any interest in the fireflies. Instead, he was asked another question about the landing bag.

Glenn was getting very curious. "Did someone report landing bag could be down?" he asked.

"Negative. We have a request to monitor this and to ask if you heard any flapping when you had high capsule rates."

Now he understood. Mission Control must be concerned about the particles after all, and they just weren't telling him.

But he was wrong. Mission Control was worried about something far more important than the mysterious lights. Unknown to Glenn, he was in the middle of a true emergency.

Back at Cape Canaveral, the landing bag warning light had lit up. It indicated that it had come loose. If it was loose, then the heat shield under it was also loose.

It was crucial that the heat shield remain on the capsule during reentry into the atmosphere. If it didn't, the capsule would have no protection from the enormous temperatures that would build up as it reentered the atmosphere.

Would *Friendship 7* return to Earth as a giant fireball?

CHAPTER ELEVEN

"Just the Normal Day in Space"

Glenn was soaring over the North American continent. There was not a cloud anywhere. From Glenn's ringside seat in the sky, he could see the Mississippi River, New Orleans, and Georgia pass beneath him. Far below, Florida looked as perfect as a map.

It was three hours and eleven minutes after launch, and Glenn was starting his third orbit. Due to the problems with automatic pilot, his seven orbits had been cut back to three. Already it was time to think about reentering the atmosphere.

From the Bermuda station, Gus Grissom recommended that Glenn use the automatic control system for reentry and back it up with manual control. Glenn pointed out that he'd had a lot of trouble with automatic control. It was going wrong in pitch, roll, and yaw. Maybe, he suggested, he better wait to make that decision.

Over Muchea, he joked with Gordo Cooper about getting his extra flight pay from the Marine Corps that month. "I want you to send a message to the commandant, US Marine Corps, Washington," he told Gordo. "Tell him I have my four hours required flight time in for the month and request flight chit be established for me. Over."

"Roger," said Cooper. "Is this flying time or rocket time?"

"Lighter than air," Glenn answered. As long as he was off the ground, the Marine Corps owed him!

Back at the Cape, a tense debate was going on. Should they tell Glenn about the heat shield warning light? There was really nothing he could do about the problem, and they did not want him worried. They decided to work on it on the ground and not bother him. They could, however, ask him to check his instruments.

Glenn did not have a heat shield indicator. But he did have a landing bag switch. The heat shield was attached to the landing bag. Both were designed to deploy after the capsule had descended through the atmosphere. Cape decided to keep asking him about the landing bag.

The Hawaii capcom informed Glenn that at Mission Control they had been reading an indication of a landing bag deploy. He asked Glenn to put the landing bag switch in auto position to see if he got a light.

Glenn was suspicious. What was it they were asking him to do? If he switched to automatic and the green light came on, it would mean that the landing bag—and the heat shield—had deployed, or been let out. And if it hadn't deployed—switching to automatic might activate it!

He was taking a chance, he knew. Still, they must know what they were doing. He rapidly switched the switch on and off. No green light. *Whew.* Everything was okay, then.

Back at Mission Control they still weren't so sure. There was only one thing they could do—ask him to keep the retropack in place.

In order to leave orbit and reenter the atmosphere, the capsule had to reduce speed. To slow it down, retrorockets on the blunt end would fire and push the capsule backwards. The rockets were held against the heat shield by heavy metal straps called the retropack. Ordinarily, to lighten the load, the retropack would be jettisoned after the rockets were fired. But if it stayed on, it might just help keep the heat shield in place, too.

Wally Schirra, in California, gave Glenn the order. "John, leave your retropack on through your pass over Texas."

Glenn still didn't get it. There was something they weren't telling him, and it was starting to annoy him. But this was no time to get angry. He was beginning the most crucial part of the mission—reentry. He had to enter the atmosphere at just the right angle. If he didn't, the capsule might bounce back into space and continue to orbit while Glenn ran out of oxygen. Or it might speed through the atmosphere too quickly and burn up. Either way, Glenn would be doomed.

He tried the automatic controls once more. For once, they seemed to work, at least in pitch and roll. The yaw was still off, so he kept one hand on the manual control. His other hand hovered over the retro-rocket switch.

Schirra started the countdown for firing the retro-rockets. "Five...four...three..."

Glenn adjusted the yaw.

"Three...two...one, *fire!*"

The three rockets fired one after the other, five seconds apart. With each explosion, Glenn felt the capsule jerk backward.

"I feel like I'm going back to Hawaii," he told Schirra.

"Don't do that," Wally joked. "You want to go to the East Coast."

The capsule sped on, slower now, moving east over

the Rocky Mountains. Texas capcom came on and directed Glenn to leave his retropack on.

Now Glenn was really angry. He was the pilot of this craft, and they were keeping vital information from him. "What is the reason for this?" he barked. "Do you have any reason?"

"Not at this time," Texas capcom said. He told Glenn that he would have to wait to speak to Mission Control.

It was up to Alan Shepard to tell him, twenty seconds later. "We are not sure whether or not your landing bag has been deployed. We feel it is possible to reenter with the retropackage on."

"Roger, understand," Glenn said.

That was an understatement. Finally he knew what they were so worried about. If he had to keep the retropack on, it must be to protect the heat shield. If the heat shield came off, he would burn up. It was that simple.

It was four hours and forty-one minutes after launch, fourteen minutes until *Friendship 7* was scheduled to splash down in the Atlantic Ocean. He had entered the upper reaches of the atmosphere. "Going to fly-by-wire again," he announced. He didn't want to take any chances with the faulty automatic system.

"We recommend that you..." Shepard said. His voice cut out. Glenn was in a communications blackout. The cocoon of heat outside the capsule would keep any transmission from getting through. For the next five minutes, during the most dangerous part of his voyage, he was on his own.

This was it, then. The astronaut heard a thump outside. "I think the pack just let go," he said to no one in particular.

The heat began to build up. Just four feet behind his back, the temperature rose to 9,500 degrees, just a little less hot than the surface of the sun. The glow outside the window was a bright orange. His back began to stiffen. If the heat shield was down, that was where he would feel the heat first.

He kept trying to contact the Mission Control. "Hello, Cape. *Friendship Seven*. Over. Hello, Cape. *Friendship Seven*..."

Silence.

Down at Mission Control, the atmosphere was tense. They had no idea whether the heat shield was up—and no way to find out.

In Arlington, Annie kept her gaze fastened on the three TVs in her living room. The Cape had phoned her to let her know there might be a problem. Now she waited.

And the world waited.

Glenn could see flaming pieces of metal fly past the window. Could that be the heat shield tearing apart? Or was it just part of the retropack?

The seconds ticked by. He waited for the first stab of heat in his back...

And waited.

It never came. Outside, the red glow began to dim. He was safe!

"A real fireball outside," Glenn said in relief.

Then the G forces began to build up, as expected, and the astronaut felt the familiar pressure thrusting him back against the seat. Now he was experiencing 7 Gs...7 1/2 Gs...

The headset sputtered and a voice came in. "...how do you read? Over."

"Loud and clear," Glenn replied.

The team at Mission Control went wild with joy. The heat shield had not burned up after all. Glenn was alive and shooting through the atmosphere, on his way to an ocean landing.

The orange-and-white parachute came out above the capsule at ten thousand feet. A few minutes later, *Friendship 7* hit the water. Astronaut John Glenn was home.

Later, after Glenn and his spacecraft were recovered, he filled out a standard NASA form about his experiences. "Was there any unusual activity during this period?" the last question on the form asked.

"No," he wrote. "Just the normal day in space."

CHAPTER TWELVE

One American Legend

America was crazy about John Glenn. When he returned to Earth from space, he was not just a hero, but a mega-hero, the most admired man in the nation. Americans loved everything about him, from his calm courage in the face of danger to his quick smile, freckled face, and solid hometown values. They were proud of their nation, proud of their astronauts, and especially proud of the man who had carried the American flag around the earth. Glenn came home to the most tumultuous and adoring welcome anyone had received since Charles Lindbergh.

Glenn got his first inkling of the media frenzy to come when President Kennedy himself made the trip to Cape Canaveral to award him NASA's Distinguished Service Medal. After the ceremony, they joined thousands of spectators in a bite of Henri Landwirth's enormous cake. It was—amazingly—still fresh!

Kennedy invited the Glenns to fly back to Washington aboard the presidential plane *Air Force One*. Annie, Lyn, and Dave were thrilled to meet glamorous Jackie Kennedy and five-year-old Caroline. It turned out that Jackie was eager to introduce her daughter to the astronaut who had gone around the Earth.

"Caroline, this is Colonel Glenn," Jackie said.

Caroline looked at the strange man and her face fell. "But where's the monkey?" she asked, obviously disappointed. Glenn, amused, retold this story many times over the next few days.

That Monday, February 26, John Glenn was invited to speak to a special joint session of Congress. Standing behind the podium in the Senate, he looked out at the country's leaders gathered before him— senators and representatives, foreign ambassadors and military officers. Then he spoke from his heart. "I am certainly glad to see that pride in our country and its accomplishments is not a thing of the past," Glenn told his audience. "I still get a lump in my throat when the American flag is passing by. Today as we rode up Pennsylvania Avenue I got this same feeling all over again. Let us hope that none of us ever loses it."

He introduced Herschel and Clara Glenn, who had traveled all the way from Ohio to be with their son in his moment of triumph. "And above all," Glenn continued, "I want you to meet the real rock in my family, my wife Annie!" The hall erupted in cheers and applause.

Washington, though, was nothing compared to New York. On March 1, 1962, John, Annie, and the six other astronauts and their wives had a ticker tape parade down Astronaut's Row, as Broadway was renamed for the day. Four million people braved 17-degree weather to greet them. They jammed the streets and leaned out of office buildings, deluging the motorcade with thirty tons of ticker tape. The enthusiasm was, Glenn said, "almost overwhelming."

Two days later Annie, John, Dave, and Lyn went back to New Concord for another parade. It was their fourth in eight days. Glenn was thrilled when his old alma mater, Muskingum College, finally granted him a college degree.

All in all, it was an exhilarating experience. But now Glenn had to decide what to do next. Naturally, he wanted to continue in the space program and participate in the upcoming missions. Perhaps someday, he thought, he could even go to the Moon.

President Kennedy, though, had already decided he should be grounded. John Glenn was a national treasure, Kennedy reasoned, far too valuable to risk in another space flight. Instead, Kennedy encouraged him to go into politics.

Eventually, that's just what Glenn did. In November 1974, John Glenn was elected to the first of four terms in the US Senate. He would serve his country for twenty-four years as senator from Ohio. During that time, he campaigned twice for the Democratic nomination for president, but never won it. Fate had a different kind of honor in store for John Glenn.

Space had never lost its pull. He had been deeply disappointed in the 1960s when NASA refused to send him back up. Ever since then, at the back of his mind had always been the thought that someday he might get another chance. Thirty years later, that chance finally arrived.

In the 1990s, NASA's space program was centered on the space shuttle. The mission of the shuttle was to repair and service orbiting satellites and to conduct scientific observations and experiments in zero-G. One day, Senator Glenn came up with a perfect shuttle experiment—an investigation of the parallels between space aging and ordinary aging.

Scientists had noticed that anyone who spent a long time in space showed many of the signs of ordinary aging—bone loss, loss of balance and coordination, immune system problems, and other things. However, no studies had ever been done on the effect of weightlessness on an older person. The men and women chosen to be astronauts were usually in their thirties and forties. No one as old as Glenn—he was seventy-three in 1995—had ever gone into space.

It was time for someone to break the record. As he later wrote, Glenn began to think, "Why not me?"

He began to bug NASA director Dan Goldin about the possibility. At first, Goldin didn't take him seriously. And Glenn's wife Annie was opposed to the idea. As he said later, the first time he brought the subject up, her reaction was less than positive. "Over my dead body!" she snapped. She didn't want anything to happen to her husband of more than fifty years. But Glenn pressed ahead. After discussing the matter again with Annie, he announced his resignation from the Senate in February 1997. And he finally overcame Annie's objections, too. As she realized how important this project was to her husband, she became more and more enthusiastic. Finally, Goldin told Glenn he could join a shuttle mission on two conditions. First, it had to be good science. Glenn's experiment really had to be of value to the scientific community. Second, Glenn would have to pass the same physical requirements as the other astronauts. So Glenn got the official "astronaut physical" at the Johnson Space Center in Houston, Texas. It was almost as tough as the one he had taken thirty-eight years before. But he passed.

On January 16, 1998, NASA made the startling announcement: John Glenn was going back to space.

He would join the crew of the space shuttle *Discovery* on a mission the following fall. This time, Glenn would not be the commander, or even the pilot, of the spacecraft. Rather, he would be the lowest ranking member of a seven-person crew, with the title Payload Specialist Number Two. His role would be to perform scientific experiments.

Glenn went to work, amazed at the changes in the space program since the 1960s. Now astronauts were not only white male test pilots, but also engineers and scientists, women, foreign citizens, and people of all races and backgrounds. The spacecraft was not a cramped 7-by-9-foot capsule, but a spacious place with a bathroom—no more rubber tubing—and a galley with hot and cold water. Instead of one squeeze tube of applesauce, Glenn and the others would have forty-two different kinds of food to choose from.

Best of all, this time Glenn would be able to really enjoy the sensation of weightlessness. He looked forward to floating around the cabin in zero-G.

On October 29, 1998, John Glenn once again found himself on the launch pad at Cape Canaveral, this time in a bright orange shuttle suit. At 2:15 P.M. the space shuttle *Discovery* lifted off, as a reporter said, "with a crew of six astronaut heroes and one American legend."

At age seventy-seven, astronaut John Glenn was back in space. Three hours into the flight, he relayed a message back to Mission Control—the same message he had sent thirty-six years earlier.

"Zero-G," he declared, "and I feel fine."

Read on for more information about
the U.S. space exploration program...

Space Explorers

"SPACE IS THE NEW OCEAN," President John F. Kennedy said in the early 1960s, "and this nation must sail upon it." The explorers of outer space, like the earlier explorers of Earth, risked everything in their journey of discovery. John Glenn and the other astronauts did not know what to expect when they left their familiar world. Would weightlessness damage their bodies? Would the vast reaches of space disturb their minds? Would their spacecraft burn up as they returned to Earth? Would astronauts sink into oceans of moon dust on the lunar surface? And what really lay on the mysterious far side of the Moon? More rocks— or another civilization?

Today we know the answers to those questions. But back when the Mercury Seven were first blasted into space on top of a

The seven original Mercury astronauts

NASA's emblem

rocket, nobody knew exactly what dangers the astronauts were facing. They dared to go anyway.

Mercury

Glenn returned from his adventure in good health and good spirits. Plenty of questions about the flight still remained, though. What about *Friendship 7*'s heat shield? Had it really been in danger of coming off on reentry? It turned out that the landing bag light had flashed on because of a signal error. The bag and the heat shield were still fastened snugly to the capsule. So Glenn was not in danger of burning up after all—but he didn't know that at the time.

Friendship 7 patch

And how about those mysterious fireflies? Scott Carpenter, who took the next Mercury flight, also noticed the same phenomenon. When he thumped on the side of the capsule, a flurry of

John Glenn practices getting into and out of the Mercury capsule.

"snowflakes" was let loose. They were bits of ice stuck to the capsule, he decided. When an astronaut's breath and perspiration were let out of the capsule through a vent, the water vapor was frozen into ice particles.

Glenn's successful flight gave the American space program the enormous triumph it needed in the early 1960s. Yet his, Shepard's, and Grissom's flights were only the first lap of a race—the race to the Moon. President Kennedy had promised that American astronauts would land on the Moon before the decade ended. Would they make it?

Deke Slayton was supposed to take the next flight after Glenn's.

But at the last moment, NASA doctors discovered that he had a heart murmur. He was dropped from the schedule.

So the Mercury torch was passed to Scott Carpenter. On May 24, 1962, his *Aurora 7* completed three orbits of Earth. On reentry Carpenter fired his retro rockets three seconds too late. The spacecraft splashed down 250 miles away from its target. For forty minutes, the world waited anxiously, uncertain whether he had survived. Meanwhile, Carpenter was lounging in his life raft and thinking about his adventure.

Wally Schirra was next, with what he called a "textbook flight" of six orbits. On May 15 and 16, 1963, the Mercury program came to a grand finale with Gordon Cooper's epic thirty-four-hour, twenty-two-orbit flight.

Mercury was a great success. It was time to take the next step.

Gemini

Getting to the Moon presented quite a challenge. NASA needed to develop an array of new technology and procedures. First, astronauts had to learn to work together for long periods of time in a confined space. Then they had to be trained to walk outside the vehicle and survive with just the protection of their pressure suits. Finally, the scientists had to develop a way for two

space vehicles to meet and dock in space. Once at the Moon, the lunar lander would leave the orbiting command module. Then it would descend to the surface, and rise again to reattach itself. If the docking procedure did not work, the astronauts would be lost—forever.

Diagram of the two-person Gemini capsule

Project Gemini, named after the twins of the zodiac, would test the new technology and skills. Designed to fit two astronauts, the Gemini spacecraft was twice as large as the tiny Mercury capsule. On each flight, NASA tested something new. On March 23, 1965, *Gemini 3*, piloted by Mercury veteran Gus Grissom and new astronaut John W. Young, experimented with changing orbits. The astronauts guided the spacecraft into higher and then lower orbits as it circled the Earth.

Next came the most exciting innovation of all—spacewalking! On June 3, 1965, astronaut Edward H. White crawled through the hatch of *Gemini 4* and climbed out into space. Connected only by a long tether, he floated alongside the spacecraft. Below him was the spectacular blue and white panorama of Earth. All around him were the planets, stars, and black space of the universe. White's space walk, which was supposed to last only twelve minutes, stretched out to twenty. Mission Control begged him to come back in, but White was having too much fun. He didn't want the walk to end. When he finally reentered the hatch, he said it was the saddest moment of his life.

Gemini patch

In the next Gemini mission, Gordon Cooper and Pete Conrad tested their endurance by staying in space for eight days. On December 15, 1965, *Gemini 6*, piloted by Wally Schirra, rendezvoused with *Gemini 7* in space. Three months later, *Gemini 8*, piloted by the talented newcomer Neil Armstrong, made space history by docking with another unmanned vehicle. Finally, after ten manned

A space walk with the astronaut tethered to the mother craft.

Gemini missions, NASA decided the program was ready. It was time to go to the Moon!

Apollo

The Apollo Project, named after the Roman sun god, was breathtakingly bold. And it started with a disaster. On January 27, 1967, the first three Apollo astronauts, veterans Gus Grissom and Edward White and rookie Roger Chaffee, were locked into the Apollo command module in the "white room" at the top of the rocket elevator. In preparation for the actual flight, they were rehearsing the countdown and launch. After five hours, NASA personnel heard a sudden cry.

An astronaut "spacewalking" with a power pack on his back.

"Fire!" Grissom's voice rang out.

Other voices chimed in. "Open 'er up... We're burning up!"

White room technicians battled the smoke and flames to open the hatch. But by the time they pried it open, all three astronauts were dead. Stunned, the nation mourned.

Apollo 8, carrying the first human beings ever to the Moon, was launched from Cape Canaveral on December 21, 1968. Three days later, Frank Borman, James Lovell, and William A. Anders went into orbit around the Moon. As they returned from the far side,

The mighty Saturn V rocket

Planet Earth

they took a photograph of an awe-inspiring sight: the Earth rising above the Moon. They were the first people to see the whole Earth, and they were struck by the beauty of our home planet.

Finally came the flight every one had been waiting for—*Apollo 11*. On July 16, 1969, Neil Armstrong, Michael Collins, and Edwin "Buzz" Aldrin blasted off from Cape Canaveral on their way to the Moon. When they reached the Moon's orbit three days later, they fired the rockets on the lunar landing module *Eagle*. The landing module detached from the command module and descended. It settled gently on the barren rock. "The *Eagle* has landed," Armstrong announced. Human beings were on the surface of the Moon!

The dark side of the Moon

Apollo 1 patch

Six and a half hours later, Armstrong and Aldrin were suited up and

The first human to walk on the moon, Neil Armstrong

ready to leave the lander. Millions of people across the globe sat glued to their TVs, watching history unfold. At 10:56 Eastern Daylight Time, July 20, 1969, Armstrong opened the hatch and climbed down the ladder. "That's one small step for man," he said when his foot touched the lunar soil, "one giant leap for mankind."

The first men had landed on the Moon just sixty-six years after the Wright Brothers flew the first airplane at Kitty Hawk, North Carolina. Forty-two years after Charles Lindbergh soared across the Atlantic. And seven years after John Glenn orbited the Earth.

America's space program would celebrate many more triumphs and also suffer more tragedies. But no achievement would ever capture the nation's imagination more than the three orbits of a tiny spacecraft called *Friendship 7* back in 1962. And no other individual astronaut would ever be more admired than the pilot of that pioneer spacecraft—John Glenn.

Comparative sizes of the space capsules: top, Apollo; middle, Gemini; bottom, Mercury. At left are the rockets that propelled each into space—l. to r., Saturn, Titan, Atlas.

**Mercury
Friendship 7
1962**

**Discovery
STS-95
1998**

Timeline of Events Following 1998 Mission on Space Shuttle *Discovery*

1998 ———• Helps found John Glenn Institute for Public Service and Public Policy at Ohio State University to encourage young people to pursue careers in civil service

1999 ———•

January
Retires from the US Senate

March 1
Lewis Research Center in Cleveland, Ohio renamed to John H. Glenn Research Center at Lewis Field

October 22
Receives Prince of Asturias Award for International Cooperation

November 2
Publishes his autobiography, *John Glenn: A Memoir*

2000 ———• Awarded US Senator John Heinz Award for Outstanding Public Service by an Elected or Appointed Official

2001 ———• Becomes Elder Statesmen, consulting President George W. Bush

2003

January
President George W. Bush appoints Glenn as an Honorary Co-chair to the President's Council on Service and Civic Participation

2004

Bestowed Woodrow Wilson Award for Public Service

2006

February
NASA awards Glenn and 37 other astronauts Ambassador of Exploration Award, recognizing the sacrifices and dedication of the Apollo, Gemini, and Mercury astronauts

July 22
John Glenn Institute for Public Service and Public Policy merges with Ohio State University's School of Public Policy and Management to become John Glenn School of Public Affairs

2008

Awarded NCAA Theodore Roosevelt Award

2009

April 22
Accepts 2008 Thomas D. White National Defense Award

June 6
Receives honorary doctorate from Williams College

2010 ———• Receives honorary doctorate of public service from Ohio Northern University

2011 ———• **November 16**
Receives Congressional Gold Medal for Distinguished Astronauts alongside Neil Armstrong, Buzz Aldrin, and Michael Collins

February
NASA awards Glenn and 37 other astronauts Ambassador of Exploration Award, recognizing the sacrifices and dedication of the Apollo, Gemini, and Mercury astronauts

2012 ———• **July 22**
John Glenn Institute for Public Service and Public Policy merges with Ohio State University's School of Public Policy and Management to become John Glenn School of Public Affairs

2013 ———• Elected to American Academy of Arts and Sciences

February 1
Attends christening of US Navy Mobile Landing Platform ship, *USNS John Glenn*

 ———• **May**
Undergoes heart valve replacement surgery

2015

April 24
John Glenn School of Public Affairs becomes John Glenn College of Public Affairs at Ohio State University

June 28
Port Columbus Airport is renamed to John Glenn Columbus International Airport

December 8
Dies at age 95 at the Ohio State University Wexner Medical Center in Columbus, Ohio

2016

December 9
Memorial held at Kennedy Space Center

December 17
Memorial held at Mershon Auditorium at Ohio State University

2017
Buried at Arlington Cemetery on what would have been John and Annie's 74th wedding anniversary, after lying in state at Ohio Statehouse

Bibliography

Carpenter, M. Scott, L. Gordon Cooper Jr., John H. Glenn Jr., Virgil I. Grissom, Walter M. Schirra Jr., Alan B. Shepard Jr., Donald K. Slayton. *We Seven: By the Astronauts Themselves.* New York: Simon and Schuster, 1962.

"The Moon. A Giant Leap for Mankind." *Time*magazine, July 25, 1969. *www.content.time.com/subscriber/article/0,33009,901102,00.html.*

Glenn, John. *John Glenn: A Memoir.* New York: Bantam House, 1999.

Godwin, Robert, ed. *Friendship 7: The First Flight of John Glenn.* The NASA Mission Reports. Burlington, Ontario: Apogee Books, 1999.

Van Riper, Frank. *Glenn: The Astronaut Who Would Be President.* New York: Empire Books, 1983.

Wolfe, Tom. *The Right Stuff.* New York: Farrar, Straus, Giroux, 1970.

For Further Reading

Bredeson, Carmen. *John Glenn Returns to Orbit: Life on the Space Shuttle.* Berkeley Heights, NJ: Enslow, 2000.

Burgan, Michael. *John Glenn: Young Astronaut.* New York: Aladdin Books, 2001.

Giblin, James Cross. *Charles A. Lindbergh: A Human Hero.* New York: Clarion, 1997.

Kennedy, Gregory P. *The First Men in Space.* New York: Chelsea House, 2001.

Kramer, Barbara. *John Glenn: A Space Biography.* Berkeley Heights, NJ: Enslow, 1998.

Nahum, Andrew. *Eyewitness: Flying Machine.* DK Publishing, 2000.

Pogue, William R. *How Do You Go to the Bathroom in Space?* New York: TOR, 1999.

Sipiera, Diane M. and Paul Sipiera. *Project Mercury.* New York: Children's Press, 1997.

For Further Viewing

The Right Stuff. Dir. Philip Kaufman. Perf. Ed Harris, Sam Shepard, and Dennis Quaid. Warner, 1983.

About the Author

Ruth Ashby has written many award-winning biographies and non-fiction books for children, including *The Amazing Mr. Franklin* and *Charles Darwin and the Voyage of the* Beagle. She lives on Long Island, New York, with her husband, daughter, and dog, Nubby.

Also by
RUTH ASHBY

Charles Darwin and the Voyage of the Beagle
HC: $12.95 | 978-1-56145-478-5
PB: $7.95 | 978-1-68263-127-0

This lively account follows the naturalist's exciting trip around the world—through seasickness, a life-threatening illness, and even an earthquake—as he explores the Cape Verde Islands, Tahiti, and the Galapagos Islands.

"Ashby makes good use of Darwin's own writings, sprinkling quotes throughout the text, which allows his adventures and opinions to come to life."
—*School Library Journal*

"[A] fascinating biography."
—*Science and Children.*

❖ Bank Street Best Children's Books of the Year; NSTA/CBC Outstanding Science Trade Books for Students K–12

The Amazing Mr. Franklin

HC: $12.95 | 978-1-56145-306-1
PB: $7.95 | 978-1-68263-102-7

The first book Ben Franklin read was the Bible at age five, and then he read every printed word in his father's small home library. Ben wanted to read more, but books were expensive. Despite this, Ben Franklin had lots of ideas about how to turn his love of reading and learning into something more. Readers follow Franklin's spirited, rebelious youth through his time as a printer's apprentice and, eventually, his higly influential career as an inventor and politician.

"An attractive and highly readable account
of Franklin's life."
—*Booklist*

❖ NCSS/CBC Notable Social Studies Trade Books
for Young People